About the author

Craig Micklewright grew up in the West Midlands and now lives in Wales. He has enjoyed writing as a hobby for much of his life and over the years has studied and developed his flair for creating worlds, characters and scenarios. He works as an I.T. Technician and is also a keen movie enthusiast. He has now published several novels that have been a realisation of a lifelong dream. Favourite genres include crime thriller & horror.

Also by

Craig Micklewright

Dying Games Saga

Showdown In Los Angeles

The Dying Game

Gemini

The Fallen

Forever Midnight

Available now at Amazon

(also available on Kindle)

The Midnight Trilogy
Book Two

iv

Reader's note:

This novel features scenes that some readers may find distressing. This includes sexual assault/abuse, as well as strong violence.

Discretion is advised.

ORIGIN

By

Craig Micklewright

Copyright © 2023 Craig Micklewright

All rights reserved. This book or any portion thereof may not be reproduced or used in any manner whatsoever without the express written permission of the publisher except for the use of brief quotations in a book review.

This book is a work of fiction. Characters, places, events, and names are the product of this author's imagination. Any resemblance to other events, other locations, or other persons, living or dead, is coincidental.

ISBN: 9798858525608

v2.6

www.craigauthor.com

Craig Micklewright

Prologue

Miami, Florida

2014

August

D etective Jim Davenport approached a door at the Miami Metro Police Department. A sign read 'morgue'. As he raised his hand, he was hesitant to enter, uncertain of his feelings. He had never experienced anything like this before. It was making him question everything he had ever known.

Entering a cold spacious room, a number of refrigeration chambers took up a far wall, closed off by large iron doors. Situated in the centre of the room, was the reason he had felt so hesitant. On a long metal table lay a body. Davenport approached, walking with a slight hunch, hair prematurely

Origin

grey in sections and the previous night's events had taken their toll. An early morning sun that beamed in from a wire-mesh window lit the table in an almost God-ray fashion.

As he stood next to the table he stared in disbelief. To all intent and purpose he was looking at the body of a young woman, albeit a decapitated one. However, it was clear she had not been entirely human, or if she had, she wasn't at the time of death. He ran his eyes over a washed, naked body, looking from the breasts to bullet holes puncturing the rib cage and abdomen, to a lightly groomed pubic area, then down long legs to where he would expect to find feet - yet in their place, were what appeared to be animal-like hooves. Flaps of split, cracked flesh hung from the ankles, like the feet had crumbled away, revealing the beast within.

On closer inspection, as Davenport leaned over the table, he noticed scaly markings running across the woman's shoulders. A transformation had clearly taken place. Whether or not she had been killed before it could complete, was unlikely to ever be answered.

Glancing to the mess of what remained of her neck, where a shotgun had removed her head, Davenport sighed both with regret and a cold uncertainty for the world he was living in. *Shit like this can end careers*, he thought to himself.

Behind him the morgue door then opened, although he didn't avert his eyes, somewhat transfixed. A small man in a white overall entered, pausing upon recognising the Detective.

"Oh sorry Sir, didn't realise anyone was in here."

Craig Micklewright

"What have you managed to extract from this?" Davenport asked.

The man approached, coming to stand beside the veteran cop. He wore glasses and had a somewhat dismissive look on his face.

"Her name was Sarah Hartshorne. 32 years of age. Employed at a local law firm. One of the partners, Montgomery Brunt was one of the victims of her erm, spree. From my examinations, she seems to be exhibiting clear signs of mutation." He replied, "Not like you know, X-Men… but possibly as a result of infection or disease. It's the only rational explanation."

Davenport turned away.

"The F.B.I get word on this I'll be up to my ears in paperwork for the rest of the year. I'll be back, but I'm tempted to just say burn it."

"Really, Sir? This could be important, for science!"

"If whatever that woman had become can be explained by science, I'll eat my badge."

With that, Davenport stormed out, leaving the man to look at the body with fascination.

In an office meanwhile, a young woman, no older than 28 lay on a sofa. She hadn't been allowed to leave; questions undoubtedly imminent now that the bodies and the carnage had likely been dealt with. Easing open her eyes to the sound of an expresso machine percolating, she sat up, muscles aching from head to toe. She looked over her shoulder to where a work surface stood before a window, a sink unit housing a wash basin piled with dishes. Next to the machine

Origin

stood a man, casually dressed in trousers and a shirt that hung loose, blonde hair ruffled as he placed a mug on the surface that read 'Me Boss, You Not' on the side.

"Darren?" She said quietly.

In her sleepiness, she mistakenly used Blake's other name. A name only she knew him by.

Immediately, he turned to look to her as her head peeked out from the back of the sofa. With the bags beneath his eyes, he looked as tired as she felt.

"Oh you're awake." He remarked, and the woman slowly stood up, legs like jelly.

She was tall with a slim waist, wearing a creased, cream coloured trouser suit, long flowing fair hair cascading down to drape her shoulders.

"Er... how are you?" She asked sheepishly and walked around the sofa to meet him.

"You called me Darren just now." He said, not answering her question and not looking at her either.

"Oh, sorry, I wasn't thinking."

"It's ok. Don't blame you. This whole thing, must have done a number on you."

The woman, her name Patricia, then reached up and touched his neck before placing a manicured hand on his cheek, forcing him to look at her. He appeared juvenile, boyish, innocent. In that moment she just wanted to hold him, but resisted the urge.

"I'm not worried about me, I'm worried about you. Do you want to talk about... last night?"

"Do I look like Rob Lowe?" He replied, looking into her wide sapphire eyes, then smirked at the reference, pulling away and returned to his coffee as the machine finished.

Patricia watched him prepare the beverage then stepped away, returning to the sofa and sitting down to put her boots on. Clearly talking about things she herself couldn't explain was pointless.

"How do you take yours?" He asked.

"These days? Black." She responded, slipping a foot into her boot then ran a zip up the one side.

The door to the office then opened, and Patricia looked over as she slipped her second foot into her other boot. Davenport then walked in, an imposing figure who Patricia had found herself befriending.

"Ah, you're awake."

"We under arrest, Detective?" Patricia then said.

"We? Er… no. Although, I'll want you to stay in reachable distance, Miss Willis. Last night raised more questions than I'm comfortable thinking about right now." - he looked down to Patricia, "You understand I'll need a statement from you. Strictly off the record, what happened could have gone much further than it did. Thankfully it was ended before that could occur."

Patricia stood up, "Want some coffee, Detective?" She asked then turned to Blake - yet he was nowhere to be seen.

"No, thank you. I'm not staying. Paperwork's a bitch." Davenport replied.

Origin

Confused, Patricia looked around the room. Blake had vanished.

"Your friend, Mr Thomas he's…"

Patricia focused on Davenport. She rubbed her head, feeling a headache coming on as she began to recall the horrors of the previous night.

"I know… how is he?" She asked quietly.

"He was catatonic when we got to him. He's had to be placed in a secure, psychiatric facility for now, for his own good."

Patricia walked over to the expresso machine, wishing what she had imagined had been real. She touched the coffee pot. It was stone cold.

"I'll leave you to get yourself together. If you'd like, I could have an officer take you over to where Mr Thomas is being held."

Patricia looked back to the Detective with optimism.

"I'd like that." She responded.

PART ONE

8

1

New York

2015

April

Blake watches her head as it moves between his legs. Lowering a small flask from his lips as he feels the warmth of her mouth, he exhales bourbon-scented breath. Looking around the untidy, unkempt room where he had been ushered, he notices pictures hanging on walls where peeling wallpaper had been put up years previous. None of the art takes his interest, his thoughts a jumble of emotions. In this very instant, he feels like he could die… yet his work has barely begun.

The woman gags slightly as she bobs her head, pausing to look up with splashed on makeup running from her eyes. She

Origin

can't be any older than eighteen … Blake doesn't care. Her mouth works and that is all that matters.

Minutes later he's zipping up his pants and heading for the door. He has left some cash on the dresser and the girl - he decides she is just a girl - sounds like she is gargling mouthwash in the bathroom. He didn't catch her name, and as he closes the door and heads off down the corridor, he begins to ponder just how long it has been since he had last stepped foot in New York. He realises it has been even longer since he had visited a 'gentleman's establishment'. However, the premises he (and at a later stage, Patricia) once owned had been turned into a brothel, so any memories he'd hoped to discover were since washed away, replaced with the stench of sex and dollar bills.

Returning to the foyer where his receptionist's desk once-upon-a-time sat, a counter now stands, behind which a middle-aged man is seated watching an old CRT TV. A news program is reporting on a forthcoming lunar eclipse. Blake pays him no attention and heads for the door, the night beckoning him - until the man speaks up.

"Hey buddy… that name you mentioned earlier." He says with a hint of tobacco-damaged lungs.

Blake turns whilst zipping up his over coat … he wants out quickly and wasn't expecting his exit to be delayed.

"What about it?" He asks, noticing an attractive blonde reporter on the TV, standing in a studio where an image of a blood red moon is displayed.

"Yeah, I know her … just didn't like the look of you before, but well, guess you're as much a paying punter as the rest of the slime balls that come around, so yeah - Juanita Equarez is the proprietor - who shall I say is asking?"

Blake steps forward out of the shadow of the doorway to be illuminated by a single fluorescent light hanging above, "Here ... give her my card. I'm not looking to cause problems for her, just a friend of a friend, in need of some answers."

The man nods and watches him leave, the rainstorm outside clearly not having calmed in the half hour or so since Blake's arrival. As silence is restored but for the lowered sound of the TV, the man turns the business card over and reads the words on the face.

'Blake Thomas – Private Detective'
followed by a cell phone number.

*

A gentle rain taps against the windscreen, wipers swishing back and forth as a man in his sixties stubs out another cigarette into an overflowing ashtray. *Harry Benning* has been in the car park of JFK International for over an hour and is tempted to start up the engine and head home... until the rear door opens, flooding the car with the cool night air. Looking over, his weathered face briefly illuminated by the lights of a passing plane, Harry sees someone sling a hold-all onto the back seat. The door closes again, and the passenger side then opens as a man in his early forties climbs in, pulling the car door closed.

Blake Thomas looks to his old friend, a man who had at one time been his mentor, but was now more like a stranger, and offers a smile. His friend has aged considerably and has

Origin

no doubt seen a lot since they were last in each other's company. But Blake has also changed and that even goes as far as his identity.

"What do I even call you these days?" Harry then asks, tired eyes examining Blake's face in detail.

Since they had last seen each other, Blake's even changed his hair colour, formerly a dark brown crew cut to wavy blonde, almost 70's-era mullet. His short goatee compliments the look, and he too has aged. That other him feels a world away from who he has become, but there's still an essence… lingering like the pungent odour of old socks.

"Blake. I've been Blake Thomas for a couple of years now. Only you and *Patricia* know that other name. Let's just say… *Darren Maitland's* long gone."

Harry let's out a sigh, looking to the windscreen as another set of lights pass overhead, "Have you any idea how many laws I'm probably breaking, just sitting here talking to you?"

"But you're retired, so drop the cop mentality, Harry."

Harry fires a look that informs Blake he isn't yet comfortable being spoken to like that.

"Let's get outta here. We'll hit a bar. Get a drink or two. I need something." He says then fires up the engine.

Blake proceeds to fix his seatbelt in place.

*

Blake hits the light switch in his bedroom and tosses his coat onto the bed… a makeshift sofa bed that hasn't been made since he crawled out of it that morning. Harry had been kind enough to allow him to stay a few nights, but he already has his eye on a small motel not that far from where he once worked as a Private Detective. Smirking at the thought of what the place had now become, he pulls his cell phone out of his pocket just as it buzzes in his hand. Flipping it open, he doesn't recognise the number, but considering present circumstances answers it anyway.

"Thomas."

"Oh hello, Mr Thomas? You left your card…" a woman's voice says with a hint of Spanish to the accent.

"Jaunita?" Blake exclaims, "Juanita Equarez?"

"How can I help you, Mr Thomas?"

"Well you see, I knew your brother… or at least I knew of him."

The woman pauses before continuing, "My brother?"

"Yes, Carlos."

Another pause, "You must be a ghost. Carlos is dead… has been for years now. Your card said you weren't five-oh, so what's this 'bout, Mr Thomas?"

"Someone I'm looking into used to work for him. I just need some information. Can we perhaps meet?"

"I'd prefer not. Who we talking about here, who are we discussing?"

"One of your brother's girls. Worked the streets over in Springdale."

"My business is a world away from what Carlo used to run, how would I have any idea who used to work for him?"

"I'm hazarding a guess you knew her. But I'd much rather meet and discuss this."

"I'm a very busy woman. The establishment you visited earlier isn't the only place I run. Just give me a name, Sir."

Origin

"Ok ok. *Lisa Ann Watts* ... does that ring any bells?"
A third pause, then the phone call abruptly cuts off.
"Hello? Miss Equarez?"

Blake curses his lack of patience and discards the phone where his coat lies, then walks into the on-suite bathroom and runs the shower. It's been a long day, exploring his old stomping ground in a quest for answers to his own problems. He's struggling to think clearly. He then begins to unbutton his shirt, and before long, steps naked under the spray and lets out a groan as the soothing warmth engulfs him.

As he stands there, hands pressed to the tiles, under the shower head ... in the background a figure moves... just a shadow... but someone for sure. Blake ignorantly continues to wallow in the spray, unaware as the shower screen slides open, until arms then slowly wrap around him. He gasps at their touch and spots a reflection of someone on the water-drenched tiles, female, a woman, and she is moving behind him, her body naked and rubbing against his. He closes his eyes tight, shaking the image of her away and quietly whispers, "No."

He is once again alone in the shower cubical, and whatever had joined him has evaporated. Gradually he reaches for the shampoo and allows his thoughts to drift back to the chat with Harry at the bar, reacquainting themselves as he drank himself into a stupor.

*

A glass of beer is placed on the counter as Harry pays the barman and watches his old friend put the cold beverage to his lips. The bar they had taken a detour to is full of winos and seedy looking characters and smells of alcohol and a hint of piss. But the fact it serves a half-decent beer is all Harry cares about. He gulps down half of his own pint then looks to Blake again.

"Let's get a booth and talk." He says then walks from the bar over to a more secluded area and sits down. He places his beer on a table as Blake takes a seat the other side.

"Patricia said you were rather messed up by what went down in Miami. If nothing else, you have my sympathy." Harry says as he begins to roll a cigarette.

Blake smiles then places his beer next to Harry's, their amber glow complimenting one another.

"You realise after a while that you're going in circles and unless you find a way of stopping the repetition, you may as well be dead. I've been dead before. It's no fun turning your back on your life, but I'd built something, Harry - thought I'd finally found happiness. But something *else* found me instead."

Harry carefully layers the tobacco then folds the cigarette paper before raising it to his lips and running the tip of his tongue over the seal. He then applies one end to a lighter and ignites the tip. Smoke and a strong smell drifts into the air once he's taken his first drag, and he glances around the bar.

"You said something on the phone about going back to where it all began. What did you mean by that… you talking about that girl? The hooker?"

Blake drinks some of his beer then nods, "Partly. But we both know it wasn't the start… that was just the final nail in the coffin of who I was back then. There's many reasons I

Origin

changed my name, made everyone think I was six feet under ... I had to become someone different entirely, but my past will always be there. I guess I just need to make sense of it."

Harry takes another drag on his cigarette, "Where you gonna start then?"

"Lisa, the girl you're referring to ... worked for a guy, some low-life pimp. He was one of her victims if you recall - one of the last. But there must be someone who's taken over his business. She was part of a big prostitution ring. Someone has to know where she came from, and who she was, before she resorted to turning tricks."

"Yeah, back then girls were getting written up all the time, Springdale especially was a hotspot for catching girls soliciting. Once that girl died, it went quiet for a year or so. The streets started cleaning up a bit and everything went into brothels and strip joints. I'll call an old buddy at NYPD... get him to give up a name. There's always someone who takes over."

Blake takes another gulp of his beer, then watches Harry take another drag and blow smoke into the air.

"Yes, that'd be good. I'll do the rest. Maybe ruffling a few feathers will knock something loose for me to grab onto. I'd like to know what really happened to her, Harry ... I'd like to know how a good person can become what she became. I know there was good in her once."

"However I can help, then. It's not like I have much else to do these days. Might be fun."

Blake nods, not exactly sure *fun* is the word he would use, "Er...yeah." He replies, then downs the remainder of his pint.

"Another?" Blake offers and gets up.

"Just a soda water for me. I'm driving, afterall." Harry responds, watching as Blake heads back to the bar.

Origin

2

Blake sits at the wheel of a grey Volvo estate, observing the building across the street that he'd once referred to as his place of business. In the light of day, it looks more familiar to him than the sleazy den of iniquity he'd sampled the previous night, but despite the passage of time the place only reminds him of his downward spiral. Blake had such clear intentions back then, overshadowed by the events that were to follow.

Shutting off the engine, he opens the door, hurrying out on spotting a middle-aged Spanish-looking woman leaving the establishment dressed in a leather jacket and embroidered jeans and heading towards a parked Mercedes. Crossing the road, Blake begins to speak as he catches up with the woman.

"Business must be booming. Nice car." He remarks as she presses a button on a key fob and the car bleeps before she opens the driver's side.

"Sorry, do I know you, Mr?" She responds, climbing in.

Blake quickly grabs the door, positioning himself between it and the car to prevent the woman closing it, "Just give me a minute. I'm not a cop. I understand that name brought back bad memories last night, but I'm after some information. Please Miss Equarez."

The woman is attractive but ageing he notices, and has a grey streak to her otherwise thick black hair, and focuses on Blake's face. *He certainly doesn't seem threatening, just desperate*, she thinks, *and a maybe a little pathetic.*

"What do you want, Mr Thomas?" She asks.

"Lisa Watts wasn't always one of your brother's girls. I just need to know where she came from. Maybe you or someone you're associated with knew her … before she began working. Before what happened, happened."

"She's dead, Mr Thomas. Why you want to bring this up now, all these years later?"

"Because sometimes… ghosts never really die."

Juanita Equarez stares at him with curiosity, then starts her engine.

"Ok, follow me. I have an office in Hell's Kitchen. Maybe I know somebody… maybe I don't. We'll see."

As Blake returns to the Volvo, across the road a young woman on a push bike comes to a halt. She is the same girl from the previous night. She recognises Blake immediately as she sits astride the bike, gripping the handle bars, her identity slightly obscured by the hood of her hoodie. She's also wearing torn, skinny jeans and sneakers. Blake left an impression. She rarely connected with her clients, but something about this guy made her feel sorry for him. The

Origin

simple fact he was still hanging around meant he was after more than just another blowjob.

*

Blake arrives at an office building a little while after, a rather shabby affair with boarded up windows in the heart of Hell's Kitchen. As he climbs out of the Volvo, he looks down the high street in reminiscence, recalling meeting with Harry at the scene of a murder a number of years back. He sighs at the memory, knowing it had begun a spiral of events that had changed everything for him.

After a moment, he reaches the third floor behind Juanita and watches as she unlocks a door.

"Just so you know, Mr… I've got a can of pepper spray on me, and I ain't afraid to use it." She warns, only semi-serious, and opens the door inwards.

A stale, musky smell is released suggesting the place hasn't exactly been attended to by a maid, a hint of old take out mixed with a myriad of other odours. Blake takes a breath and follows the woman inside.

"My dear old brother used to keep some documents in a cabinet, girls who used to work for him. When did you say it was?"

"Seven years back. 2008." Blake replies, passing by a kitchen where good to his presumption, unwashed dishes and pizza boxes are piled on the drainer.

They enter a room that is made out to be an office, with a large oak desk over by one wall and tons of paperwork piled

20

towards the ceiling. A large, shabby-looking poster hangs on a wall of a bare breasted woman.

"I think I have some stuff in this cabinet here, feel free to look through it."

Juanita steps aside to reveal a steel filing cabinet and Blake approaches. She then walks back to the doorway, propping herself against the framework as she takes out a pack of cigarettes and sparks up. Blake had noticed the gold bangles that hang from one wrist, the large drop earrings on her ears and her perfume smells like she bathes in it. *She's obviously compensating*, he muses, *due to her gradually fading youth.*

"So, what gives? Are you like, some old John of that girl? I take it you heard the stories…"

Blake pulls open the top drawer and begins to run his fingers over the hanging files, which lie coated in dust.

"Depends on what you mean by stories."

"That she killed some folk."

Blake glances over to her briefly, then continues perusing the files.

"At the time it was everywhere. The papers labelled her some sort of serial killer. Not something you really hear a woman labelled as."

"Lisa wasn't a serial killer, at least not in the usual sense."

"Oh, why? What you know about her? I wasn't that acquainted with my little brother at the time… but, I can't say I was all that surprised when I found out he got himself offed."

"You wasn't?"

"Carlo was no Angel. I'm fully aware of that, but doesn't mean he deserved to go the way he did."

Origin

Blake retrieves a brown file and turns it over. It's dated February 2008. On opening it he finds a photo that immediately causes him to shudder. It's a rather crude picture of a girl with dark hair, seemingly taken in the office he now finds himself standing in, going by the same bare-breasted poster, looking brand new - on the wall behind. He runs a finger over the image as a myriad of emotions stir within him.

He looks over to Juanita, "Can I take this?"

Juanita shrugs her shoulders, "Go ahead. I was planning on throwing that shit out months back when I took over. Guess you turning up gives me the kick to finally do it."

Blake grabs the file and slides the cabinet shut with a loud clunk. He then goes to pass Juanita until she grabs him by the arm. She locks her eyes with his.

"Just… don't come back. As far as that whore and my brother is concerned, they're both dead and buried in the past."

Blake recognises the seriousness in her eyes and appreciates he has asked more than enough just coming here. He decides a swift exit is the best course of action.

*

Blake slams the file on the table as he and Harry sit in Harry's living area. His apartment seems to yell the fact it's lived in by a single male who has mostly given up on maintaining appearances; discarded take-out packets and plates, an ash tray filled to overflowing with cigarette stubs, wallpaper that has become discoloured from the cigarette smoke.

"What's this?" Harry enquires, looking like he just crawled out of bed, his thinning grey hair untidy and is wearing a dressing gown, pyjamas just visible underneath.

"Seems Carlos kept some records on the girls who used to work for him." Blake replies, then opens the file to reveal the photo of Lisa.

"Damn…" Harry remarks.

"What?"

"I forgot how pretty she… was."

"There's an address, over on Staten Island. Not that bad a neighbourhood if I recall." Blake adds, "I know what the media said and the case notes, hell I was there… I lived it but, Harry… this isn't the face of a killer. If what I saw in Miami was anything to go by, there's more to this whole thing. It got a hold of Sarah, made her do what she ended up doing … but it started with Lisa."

Harry looks to Blake, never entirely comfortable with the whole 'otherworldly forces' possibility, but is willing to play along, at least to see where it leads.

"So, what's your next play?"

"We take a trip over to Staten. See if anyone remembers her and is willing to talk. Then maybe, see where they buried her. I haven't really said goodbye in the whole seven years, Harry… it could be a way of finding some closure, or at least a start to some closure."

"Seven years is a long time. Maybe her folks have moved on?" Harry comments.

"I guess we'll find out." Blake says then gets up, grabbing the file and walking out of the living area.

Harry is quick to follow.

Origin

*

Juanita Equarez is finishing a glass of red wine whilst sitting at a desk in her office. That man's sudden appearance has troubled her, much more than she expected. Anyone asking after Carlo was likely to do that, but the fact he mentioned 'her' really got under Juanita's skin. She opens a book, a scrap book of sorts that has a number of newspaper clippings crudely glued to the pages. One headline reads: 'twelve women found dead in hotel room'. She turns the page, and another headline reads: 'Eight year old girl dies following satanic cult abduction'. She places her wine down then picks up a cigarette, bringing little more than a stub to her creased, chapped lips and takes a final drag before squashing the cigarette out in an ash tray.

She then leafs back through several pages, and lands on a page with somewhat older looking clippings. These are worn with frayed edges, somewhat faded. They appear to be crime-scene photos, and one depicts a bald headed, Spanish-looking man. He's mostly covered up with a sheet whilst lying in the centre of a large painted pentagram.

Quickly she grabs her cell phone and brings up a list of contacts. Scrolling through the names with her thumb, she lands on one called 'Drago'. She hits the call icon.

After a moment the other end answers.

"Didn't I say I was doing that thing today?" Comes a gruff voice.

"Hey, Drago. I know, sorry but this really can't wait. I think we might have a development."

"I'm listening."

With that, Juanita closes the scrap book, then picks up Blake's business card, looking at his name with curiosity.

Origin

3

Miami

2014

As Patricia Willis travelled in the passenger seat of a Police squad car, she couldn't help but mull over the decisions which had led her to leave the safety and comfort of her family back in Los Angeles, to return to a career she'd once walked away from. She wasn't certain moving to Miami had been the best idea considering all that had occurred, however like it or not, she was now along for the ride. She glanced to the sun-tanned officer at her side, a man she hadn't spoken to before, who had been there when the shit hit the fan. He was lucky to be alive - they all were.

"So, you and this guy, you work at the same place?" The officer asked.

He was not bad looking, Patricia mused, and looked to be in his early thirties.

"Yeah, I only moved here a couple of weeks back. It's been well... crazy to put it mildly."

"I er... lost some good friends last night. I still don't understand what went down. What the hell was that? Was that woman crazy or something?"

"Or something." Patricia replied, not really able to put into words what herself and several others had been witness to.

At the psychiatric facility, Patricia was escorted down a corridor by a large Matron carrying a clipboard. She was apprehensive to see her friend, nervous of what state he might be in. The last time she was with him he was a mess, crying uncontrollably as she held him in her arms after he had just killed the woman he loved. She began to wonder if this latest event was going to be the one to finally destroy him. Although the Police didn't act like he was being charged. In all truth, it had been self-defense, and prevented an estimated body count in double figures, from turning into a full-on massacre.

Patricia followed the Matron into a lounge area where a number of patients were located. Some played board games together, others sat watching a TV positioned up high out of reach on the wall. She noticed Sandra Bullock on the screen wearing an astronaut suit as she floated in space.

Over by a window, which had bars on the outside, seated in an armchair was Blake. Patricia turned her attention to him,

Origin

immediately making her approach. Blake sat staring out to the grounds, inaccessible but a view none the less, framed with overhanging palm trees. As Patricia came to his side, he did not seem to notice. She sat down on a wide window sill, and looked at him. He failed to make eye contact.

"Blake?" She said softly.

Damn he looks far gone, she thought - his eyes devoid of the personality she knew he bestowed. Something had died inside, that much was obvious.

"Blake..." - she reached forward and took his hand, "Blake, it's me... it's Patricia."

She sighed, holding his hand tightly. He was warm to the touch, wearing a dressing gown and pyjamas, slippers on his feet. He was a sorrowful sight.

"I'm so sorry this happened, Blake. I'm sorry you had to go through that. But it's over now. I'm here. I'm going to make sure you come through this and find yourself again. Get back to who you are. Back to being a detective. Back to being..." - tears welled up in her eyes, "... my friend. I'm hurting too, Blake. But I'll be strong... for you, we got a deal?"

She leaned forward and embraced him.

"It'll never be over." He then mumbled as she cradled his head against her.

She moved back looking at him sternly.

"What was that?"

Blake's eyes focused on her, "It'll never be over." He repeated, before looking away again.

The Matron re-appeared, and Patricia turned her attention to her.

"Time for his meds." The large, imposing woman announced.

"What you got him on?"

"Oh, just something to relax him. He was very worked up when he arrived. The doctor has him on a medication that helps."

Patricia looked from the Matron to Blake again.

"Hey, I bought some of your things with me. If you want to talk, just call me anytime." She said, retrieving Blake's cell phone and wallet from within her jacket and placing them on the window sill.

His expression had become vacant once more. She stood up.

"I'll leave you be for now, but think about what I said, alright?" She concluded and walked away as he failed to respond.

As she walked back out of the lounge area, she found herself starting to weep. Damn it, she felt at a loss how to help him. Perhaps time was going to be his only healer. With that thought, she proceeded down the corridor, quickening her pace as she yearned to leave the place and return to the outside world.

As Patricia emerged from the facility, a humid heat beating down, she approached the awaiting squad car, only to see two men dressed in black suits chatting with the tanned officer. Then to her surprise, the squad car pulled away and drove off down the street. Patricia reached the suited men, looking at them with confusion.

"Hey, what's going on?" She asked.

Origin

The one man produced a wallet, briefly flashing an I.D. "Connor Wilson, FBI."

Patricia just focused on the man, bemused.

"Sorry to bother you ma'am. We have reason to believe you were witness to an 'incident' last night. If you don't mind, we'd like to have you come with us for an informal chat."

"This the point where I say no, but you taser me or some shit, then I'm never heard from again?"

The other man chuckled, "Someone has been watching too many movies."

"I promise we won't keep you long. Then we can give you a lift right back to your place of residence. That's how nice we are."

Patricia sighed.

Eventually, she sat in a diner opposite the two agents. She added two heaped spoonfuls of sugar to a black coffee, then stirred the spoon slowly.

"What we believed you witnessed last night, Ms Willis was a class 37 anomaly. That's agency speak, you understand." Agent Wilson began.

"It's fine. I've seen X-Files." Patricia quipped, and briefly recalled a man named David confessing his love for the show.

The other agent smiled.

"Our investigation is to be going through all Police files connected to the incident to see if we can come up with any answers. The fact we're dealing with something the average person can't understand means anything we come up with will remain classified."

"And that means?"

"To put it bluntly, you're not to discuss any of what you saw, or didn't see more to the point, with anyone."

Patricia took a sip of her coffee. She really didn't give a damn and was just thinking of Blake.

"Also, we will require complete access to any files at the detective agency you work at."

Patricia looked at them, "Really? I'm not sure we have anything useful."

She then recalled placing a transparent pentagram over a map of Miami.

"Well, we will be the judge of that. Your co-operation could be valuable to our investigation. Will the owner be around?"

Patricia looked away, observing a family celebrating what looked to be a birthday, going by the balloons and a huge cake before a teenage girl. She briefly pictured David as he lay over her, moving his body in time with her own and her kissing him. A tear welled up in her eye.

"Ms Willis?" Agent Wilson said.

"You know, for people who act so well informed, you'd think you would know that the owner of the agency was murdered... by that... woman. Jeez, isn't his brother your boss or something?"

The other agent checked a note pad that he retrieved from within his suit jacket, "Forgive us, Ms Willis. Yes, that's correct, *David Henderson* was one of the victims. Excuse us. Section Chief Henderson's our senior."

Patricia got up, looking exasperated.

Origin

"The way I see it, you can't arrest me or nothing so, come over to the agency. Do what you have to, but I've got other matters I need to deal with."

She then tossed a couple of bucks on the table and walked away.

The two agents looked at each other, until Wilson called after her.

"Ms Willis, what about that lift?"

"I'll get a cab." She shouted back as she exited the diner.

*

That night, Blake was lying in bed. His mind was so utterly wired he couldn't be sure if it was the medication or just how he was feeling. He tossed and turned within a thin, barely adequate sheet, before finally lying on his back staring at the ceiling. His eyes were not even heavy like they normally would be. He sat himself up slightly, patting the pillow down and positioning it behind him. He grabbed his wallet from where it sat on a bedside cabinet next to his cell, and as he opened it up, a photo was revealed in a compartment on the left-hand side. Looking across the room, the shadows on the walls and the hint of moonlight bleeding in from a window, made all around him look eerie, the silence only adding to his unease.

Focusing on the photo, it depicted his fiancé, Sarah. Taken in better times… before it all went wrong… before her death. He ran one finger over the image of her, the photo taken on the beach, the two of them in a loving embrace. As he looked at the image, he then gasped as she turned her head and grinned directly at him.

Dropping the wallet, which tumbled off the side of the bed and landed on the floor, Blake sat up with a start. *What the hell?* He thought.

Just then a child-like chuckle was heard. Looking beyond his bed to the dark shadowy corner of the room, to his continued horror he noticed a figure, standing there but not initially definable.

"Who is that?" He asked out loud, needle-pricks of goosebumps awakening all over his body.

A bare leg then stepped forward, revealing a hoofed foot that clicked on contact with the tiled floor. Blood trickled down from several loose strands of skin around the ankle. It was the same for her other leg, hoofed and with torn, hanging flesh. Blake gasped. The figure then walked forward, it's arms slightly raised as long strings protruded from the wrists, and finally Sarah moved forward like a marionette, appearing to be held up by a number of strings coming from somewhere above.

"Sarah?" Blake remarked in disbelief and abject terror.

She hobbled awkwardly as if she was being controlled by an unseen puppeteer, a slightly anorexic body wobbling as she moved, and she had a stupid fixed grin on her face.

"No… you're not real! You're dead!"

Sarah reached the bedside, and Blake noticed she was naked but for long white hair hanging down to partially cover her breasts. Streaks of blood painted themselves all over her body. Slowly she reached her hand out and beckoned him with a 'come hither' of her bony finger. She turned and

Origin

walked awkwardly over to the door, then opened it, light flooding the room as the sound of screams and gunfire spilled inside. Despite his reservations, Blake climbed from his bed, treading the cold floor with bare feet, and followed.

Exiting his room, he found himself in a corridor that was horribly familiar. He was back at the Police station. Several bodies littered the floor, blood smearing the walls. He watched Sarah walk ahead and disappear around a corner. Quickening his pace, he reached the far end and peered into the next corridor to see... himself, confronting Sarah whilst holding a shotgun. A couple of officers stood a few feet away, guns in their hands but hesitant to shoot ... just waiting, like Blake was, to see what he would do. Then a loud blast shattered his ear drums, resulting in the total obliteration of Sarah's head, and her deformed, barely human body dropped to the floor.

Blake turned away and buried his head in his pillow - back in his hospital bed, "No. Please! Sarah!!"

A hand then came to his shoulder. He turned to discover a young nurse standing by the bed looking concerned.

"Mr Thomas? You were having a nightmare!" She said.

Blake looked around the room. It was morning. Gradually he calmed himself. It had been a dream, brought on by events he knew were going to stay with him for a long time, if not forever. Looking to the young nurse's face, even her concerned expression was of little comfort.

4

New York
2015

s clouds gather in the sky, threatening further rain, Blake walks ahead of Harry as they proceed down the street of a suburban neighbourhood on Staten Island.

"So, tell me, how's Patricia been doing?" Harry asks, now fully dressed, struggling to keep up.

"Patricia?" Blake responds, looking slightly troubled by Harry's question, "Last I saw, she was erm, tip-top."

"She text me about the baby. Came as a bit of a shock."

"Well, I put off coming back here until the kid arrived. After I left hospital, I had to get the agency back on its feet following what happened to David, the owner. All of that nearly finished the place; the bad press, the Feds and the

Origin

Police poking their noses in. At least these days the agency mostly runs itself."

Blake pauses outside a gate with stereotypical white picket fencing and looks to a small bungalow. He takes out a notepad from his coat, checking the address.

"This is it, 52a Mulberry Lane." He announces.

Harry rings a doorbell, and a shadow is soon seen behind a screen door. The inner door then opens to reveal a middle-aged woman in an apron, holding a duster like she's in the midst of cleaning.

"Can I help you?" She asks, still behind the screen.

"I'm sorry ma'am, do you have a few minutes? I promise you we're not cops. It's about someone who used to reside at this address…" Harry replies.

Soon Harry and Blake are sitting on a sofa that's still wrapped in plastic dust sheets. It squeaks and crumples as they move. Looking around the rather ordinary suburban living room, Blake notices a photo on a wall of a young girl, seemingly at some majorette competition going by the green and white uniform, and she's holding a baton.

The woman returns carrying some cups with saucers. On closer inspection she looks in her late fifties.

"I'm sorry gentlemen, I'm all out of cookies." She says as she places the cups of tea down.

"It's fine Miss, please, won't you take a seat?" Harry says, "We promise we're just going to ask a few questions, then be on our way."

36

The woman sits down on the edge of an armchair with a coffee table separating herself from the two men.

"I know this can't be an easy thing to talk about, but we're here about Lisa Watts. We have information she used to live at this address."

The woman's face instantly looks troubled, as if the mere mention of that name disturbs her.

"Lisa was er… my niece. Her folks moved away a few years back, after what happened. They kind of got blacklisted in the neighbourhood."

"I'm sorry to hear that, Miss." Blake then adds, picking up his tea and taking a sip.

"I was looking for a property at the time, and agreed to help them out. I'm not so bothered by gossip. I've lived here alone ever since."

"We are simply looking into Lisa's upbringing, her former years before things went bad." Blake continues.

"May I ask something? How did you know Lisa?"

Blake isn't sure how to answer. Fortunately, Harry answers for him, "I'm a retired Lieutenant of the NYPD homicide division. I suppose you could say, I'm looking into a few old cases that remain open. A little information can go a long way to understanding exactly what transpired."

Harry pulls out his wallet and briefly flashes an I.D. stamped with 'retired 'over his photo.

Blake can't help but feel relieved.

"I er… think there's some of Lisa's things in the basement. I never felt right throwing them out and well, her

Origin

mother was kind of in a hurry to leave. There'd been death threats, you know."

"That's awful, Miss." Blake pipes up.

The woman looks at him, smiling with her eyes, "Call me Mandy, please."

She then gets up, walking out of the living room, "Follow me, gentlemen."

Blake feels fortunate that this woman is so trusting – they could be anyone, he ponders, and fake I.D. these days are dime a dozen.

A light is switched on in the bungalow's basement, illuminating a steep set of stairs. Mandy leads the way as Harry and Blake follow. It's stereotypical of spooky basements. Blake tries not to jump to conclusions that they could find a body or get attacked by the Babadook.

Once they reach the basement, it's a large spacious area with boxes, DIY tools, two old vacuum cleaners, various suitcases – but is otherwise tidy and fairly clean. Mandy is clearly someone who takes pride in her housework, given away by the apron and duster on first appearance. Blake wanders around, noticing a bookshelf with rows upon rows of paperback novels.

"Oh, I used to be a writer some years ago. I wrote children's stories. I haven't really had the flair for it in recent times however, not since my illness."

"Illness?" Harry remarks.

Mandy approaches one large crate and prizes the lid off, peering inside, "Yes, I had breast cancer when I was fifty-

38

three. Double mastectomy. All in the past now but well, it did a number on me. Not been able to write a word since."

She then took out a high school yearbook and placed it to one side, followed by some other books, magazines as well as items of clothing.

"This was all Lisa's. She was in the majorettes, you know."

"Oh, was that Lisa when she was younger, in that photo on the wall of your living room?" Blake asks as he handles a spade with curiosity.

"Yes. She came first place that year. She was thirteen. She was such a sweet child and model pupil up until about a month after that photo was taken. Her parents put it all down to 'the terrible teens', you know, boys and such."

Blake leans the spade against a wall then approaches the crate, picking up the yearbook and opens it to a random page, laying eyes on the various smiling faces. He had despised school himself and was never one of the popular guys. He had also been bullied quite extensively. His head hurt just thinking about it.

"Her picture is on page 12." Mandy adds.

He flicks through the pages, then lands on page twelve. Immediately he recognises which one is Lisa, even before reading the name. The pretty but serious looking girl with long dark hair. Although he only knew her a short time and several years after she left high school, her beauty was just as evident. Looking at her now, he just yearned to know what had happened, how things could have gone the way they did.

Harry has picked up one of Mandy's novels and is looking through it with interest. Every other page seems to have illustrations of animals dressed in human clothing.

Origin

She then holds up a t-shirt with a logo of the band 'Green Day' printed on it.

"Lisa loved rock music. She went to this one's concert when they were in the city. She used to say it was the best day of her life."

Blake nods, not doubting it for a second.

Harry then walks over, novel clutched in his hand, "You seem like you were around a lot during Lisa's life. Am I right to presume Lisa's mother is your sister?"

"Yes, Lisa's mother, 'Susan' and I are sisters. We haven't really had much to do with one another in recent years. I think she just wants to find a way of carrying on. As Lisa's auntie though, I used to help out. Susan was working two jobs back then. This is quite a nice neighbourhood, so rent's never been cheap and after Lisa's father, 'Mike' took off ... things got hard. I'd made some money as a children's author so was in a good position to lend a hand. I'm the main reason Lisa went to a good school."

Blake then noticed a photo as it fell out from between the pages. It was a family photo going by the teenage Lisa. Two older people stood behind her, a small woman standing next to a large, imposing looking man who had both hands on Lisa's shoulders. Standing slightly away from the others, was a young boy.

"Oh, is this Lisa's brother? Joseph was his name, am I right?" Blake then asks, running a finger over the face of the scrawny, loner-looking boy.

Harry looks to him, all too aware of how things ended for that guy, and the rumours surrounding him.

Mandy's cheerful expression immediately changes.

"Joseph? Oh, he was erm… not part of the household. He had an illness when he was young and mostly stayed in institutions. I er… didn't have much to do with him, neither did their mother. I'm sorry, I'd rather not discuss the matter if that's alright."

"May we ask, is Lisa buried around here? The local cemetery?" Harry asks, quick to change the subject as he replaces the novel on the bookshelf.

Mandy turns back to the crate, placing items inside. Blake hands back the yearbook, and she places it amongst the other things, before returning the lid. Whilst her back is turned, Blake conceals the photo in his coat pocket.

"I think I have the er… exact location." Mandy then replies, "They buried her at a cemetery over in Brooklyn. Er… I'll just see if it's in the dresser. Follow me."

Mandy sees the two men out of the front door as Harry thanks her for the cemetery details.

"You have been a great deal of help." Harry says holding a piece of paper in his hand.

"You know…" Mandy then says, "I realise I clammed up just now, when you brought up Joseph. The family are all too aware of what people have said. Lisa left home here not long after he came out of hospital. If you really want to find out what went on, I'd begin by looking into Joseph. There's nothing of that boy's things here, but well, he had an apartment with a girl he knew, over in Springdale."

Origin

Blake smiles at her, agreeing Joseph could indeed be significant.

"Thank you, Mandy. We'll be sure to look into that." He assures, then walks down the path towards the bungalow gate.

"You take care of yourself." Harry then adds, touching her arm briefly before turning away.

Mandy watches them go, slowly stepping back inside and closes the door.

5

2014

September

Blake looked around the room. It was a nice enough office. Certainly more impressive than his own room or anywhere else he'd seen at the institute. The man behind a large oak desk was one of the senior psychiatrists. Clearly, Blake observed, this was the guy who decided if you were well enough to leave, or if it was time to throw away the key.

"So, Mr Thomas. How long has it been since you came to us?"

Blake looked at him, noticing his balding scalp, how his horn-rimmed glasses balanced precariously on the bridge of his nose. He was probably in his late-fifties, had letters after his name no doubt.

Origin

"Has it been a month?" He answered.

The man checked a file, opening it and turning pages.

"This will be week five. So, how are you feeling? When you joined us, you were rather unwell, you might say, hysterical."

Blake straightened the collar on his dressing gown. He didn't like how this man analysed him.

"Much better, Doc." He replied.

The man checked the file again, "As I recall, not long after you arrived, you were insisting to the nurses and orderlies, that you were seeing your fiancé, Sarah - er, the woman you killed at the Police Precinct. You gave the impression she was haunting you."

Blake bowed his head, looking at his hands, "Like you just said... I was hysterical."

"That's all stopped, then? Tell me Mr Thomas, you don't see your fiancé now, do you?"

Blake sighed then slowly raised his head. Looking straight ahead he focused on the man, and standing beside him was the naked form of Sarah, her body still stained with blood, her hair bright white, and she was grinning like a Cheshire Cat.

"No... I don't. She's gone." He lied.

The man began to make notes as Sarah just stared, seeming to mock Blake's very existence.

"So, it says here, that you have responded well to the medication. No more night terrors, and you've been taking part in activities. The nurses have said your behaviour has greatly improved. Do you think you're better, Mr Thomas?"

"Well, put it this way, Doc… after a while you learn to live with your demons."

"What do you mean by that?"

Blake looked to Sarah again. She was still grinning.

"Either that or you go crazy. I'm not crazy Doc."

The man began to scribble on a pad, then tore a page off.

"I'm prescribing you a two-week course of your medication, Mr Thomas. I'd recommend staying on them for now. Then perhaps seek some therapy. You experienced a traumatic event that really affected you. Other than that, I can't see why you can't be discharged."

*

About an hour later, Blake reached the door of his apartment. He raised his hand and inserted a key in the lock, turning it and pushed the door inwards. It felt like more than a year since he'd been there, even if it had only been weeks. He squinted as the Florida sun bled into the hallway from an open door leading to a living area. He checked a watch on his wrist, then kicked the door shut, placing a plastic bag with some toiletries and clothing on a side table. He half expected Sarah to come hurrying out of the kitchen to greet him. On this occasion however, he was relieved the 'Sarah' he had been witness to, was absent.

"Patricia?" He called.

He walked into the living area, glancing around. Damn, the place was immaculate – and was that a brand-new drinks cabinet? Minus any actual alcohol it seemed. He noticed a window was open, and there was a smell in the air of recently

Origin

cooked breakfast - bacon if he wasn't mistaken. He then heard a toilet flush and turned, looking back to the hallway just in time to see Patricia walk out of a bathroom, wearing a baggy t-shirt and socks. She was startled as she looked over and spotted him. She was holding something in one hand.

"Blake!" She exclaimed, and he approached.

They met up in the doorway, and Blake went to hug her then saw what was in her hand.

"Hey, isn't that a…"

She looked at him like she'd just been caught stealing candy, then glanced at the small device… it was a pregnancy test.

"I… erm, I'm late and I've been having some nausea."

"What? Really? What does it say?"

Patricia looked at the test, then noticed a blue line next to a + symbol. She let out a gasp.

"I'll have to see a doctor but, guess this means I'm pregnant!"

"Pregnant? How??"

Patricia looked at him and screwed her face up as if to say 'really?'. She then wandered into the living area and reached a table by a window. Curtains swayed in a breeze; a view of the city slightly obscured.

"I mean, you know… I wasn't aware you'd been with anyone." Blake stammered.

Patricia sat down, handling the tester for a second then placed it before her. Blake reached the table, looking to her with concern.

"After what happened, I wasn't going to say anything, but…"

Blake frowned, "What you talking about?"

Patricia looked at him as her eyes welled-up with imminent tears.

"David. We kinda, well… we slept together."

"When??"

"In the middle of all that stuff, we were drinking one night, at the office and one thing…"

"…led to another. Jesus Christ, Patricia."

"Yeah, I know... Shit. I never thought this would happen to me, not again."

"Again?"

Patricia bowed her head, pausing before she spoke, "When I was in London… it's hazy now, but I think I was involved with a guy. He got me pregnant, but during my stint in prison, I was attacked, and lost the baby. I thought that was my one and only chance."

Blake was shocked. Clearly, he hadn't learnt as much about Patricia as he thought, leading up to contacting her again back in July. He leaned against the table and touched her hand. She looked up to him then pulled her hand away, standing back up.

"I'll er… need to get checked out, to make sure but… it's David's. There's been nobody else."

"Hey, Patricia. I'm here for you, if you decide to keep it."

Patricia froze, then glanced back, "Are you serious? I would never get rid of it. This is a blessing, Blake… else it wouldn't have happened. This way I can continue David's legacy… he can continue as part of this child."

Blake smiled at the idea, "I understand. You want I take you to the medical centre?"

Origin

Patricia looked at him then walked away, "Give me a minute. I'm still processing all this." She answered, walking out to the hallway.

Blake watched her venture back into the bathroom, the faucet running seconds after as he followed, but lingered outside.

"Enough about me. So, why didn't you call? I could've come pick you up." Her voice continued, slightly raised.

"The Doc had me in for a review and gave me this spiel about how well I've been doing and such. And so, he discharged my ass. It was kind of all of a sudden."

He heard the water go off, then Patricia returned to the hallway, immediately wrapping her arms around him.

"I'm so glad you're out of that place."

Blake rested his chin on her shoulder, nose nuzzling her long fair hair as she squeezed him against her. She smelt of lavender.

"Me too, Patricia, me too." He said and closed his eyes tight as he returned her embrace.

Patricia gradually pulled away, "So, how are you doing? You're looking well." She remarked, her wide eyes looking into his with affection.

Blake looked around then wandered back into the living area. He approached an expensive looking two-seater leather sofa and flopped down.

"Easy enough to feed those quacks a line or two so I'm not stuck in that head shrinking hole for the rest of my life."

Patricia came and stood next to the table. Blake looked over to her and noticed how her t-shirt rose up a little as she ran one hand back through her hair, revealing a glimpse of white underwear, her long legs toned. He forced himself not to stare.

"How do you mean?" She asked.

He smirked, "Nothing. So, how's the agency doing? I'm kind of eager to get back there."

Patricia looked dismissive of his question, "There's a few cases we're working on but, I don't know… are you really ready?"

Blake looked down to some books and leaflets on a small coffee table before the sofa. He reached forward and ran his hand through them. One was a flyer for an organisation called 'Sect of the Fallen Angel'.

"What's this?" He asked.

Patricia looked back, then her expression changed as she noticed him reading the flyer.

"Satanism?" He then added, "Patricia, do you have something to tell me?"

Patricia hurried over and snatched the flyer out of his hand.

"Sorry, I should have put that stuff away. I was up last night looking into it."

"You were, why?"

Patricia sighed realising she couldn't keep such things from Blake's detective brain.

"Ok, Listen. After what happened, I started looking into that cult, you know, the women who all died and seemingly brought back… well, you know…"

Blake looked disturbed, "Just sit down and tell me." He urged.

Patricia took a seat in an armchair opposite.

Origin

"Those women, new evidence has come to light to suggest they were connected to this religious organisation. For a while now there's been a kind of uprising, of alternative religious groups that follow the image of Satan, you know, the devil."

"Ok… we kinda figured that from the off. Nobody kidnaps an eight year old and attempts to sacrifice the poor kid if they're God fearing Christians."

"There's a shit load of stuff on the internet about them with their churches or whatever is the devil-worship equivalent, sprouting up all over the states. Yet most people, Police, Feds think they're just harmless kooks."

"Harmless until they resurrect a malevolent demon." Blake quipped.

"Most stuff I've looked into, in order to find a face to the outfit, has come up as a dead end. So, I was swatting until about 2a.m. last night trying to figure out my next step."

"Our next step."

"I dunno, Blake. This could be too soon, after Sarah."

Blake relaxed back, putting one foot up on the coffee table, "I'll be the judge of that. Let me see everything you got on this freak show."

Patricia just stared at him, not entirely comfortable having Blake back onboard just yet, if at all. He had been a partner in the agency though, so she was never going to be able to keep her findings from him indefinitely.

"Alright. I'll put some clothes on, and we'll head over to the agency." She replied, then got up and walked away.

Blake just focused on the flyer again. The organisation's logo depicted that of a black goat with prominent horns. The image was enough to send chills down his spine.

6

Patricia and Blake walked through the main office of H&T Investigations as various staff approached, surprised to see Blake.

"It's so good to see you, Blake. Welcome back." one young black girl said and greeted Blake with a kiss to his cheek, squeezing his arm.

"Thank you, Anna, it's good to be back."

"How you feeling, Sir?" Another guy asked, as Blake followed Patricia into an office that used to belong to David.

"Better, Richie, Thank you." He answered and turned, closing the office door to a growing crowd, and with relief shut out the noise.

"Jesus." He remarked, a little overwhelmed as he watched Patricia, now wearing a black business suit consisting of a tight jacket and knee-length skirt, walk over to David's desk.

Origin

"They've all been so concerned." She commented, turning around and resting against the front of the desk.

Blake stared at her admiringly. *She certainly looks the part,* he thought, *and grants the agency a sophistication it mostly lacks.*

"You look great." He said without thinking.

Patricia smiled, the morning sun coming in from the window making her golden hair shimmer.

"I took the liberty of moving in here after what happened. I didn't have my own office. Hope you don't mind."

"It's fine. Er… how was the funeral? Sorry I wasn't there. I could never have handled it."

"It was er… fine. His brother was there, and well, a few locals and most of the guys here, but that was it. The press was also hanging around, like fuckin' vultures … picking over what was left of David's life."

Blake approached, coming to stand close to her and took both her hands in his own, "David he… he was a special person. A good friend."

Patricia bowed her head, feeling emotions build up. She nodded.

"He was." She agreed, moving away, and Blake watched as she approached a filing cabinet.

"I guess there's a lot to sort out, what with David's share of the business. I certainly won't be able to handle all that myself."

Patricia pulled open a drawer in the cabinet and took out a file, "Well, I've been thinking about all that. I understand, without David, things could get financially strained going forward. So… I have a proposal."

She walked behind the desk and sat down in a leather chair. The window behind painted a pinstripe shadow over her as the sun bled through the blinds.

She pushed the file to one side, and leaned forward, clasping her hands together as she rested on her elbows.

"I've got money, you know that…"

Blake walked forward, resting one ass cheek against the front of the desk, looking down at her. He knew where this was going and, in many ways, it was a relief as much as he also wanted to say no.

"I can buy David's stake in the business, if you want me to. In fact, it would be an honour."

She looked hopefully to him with her striking, sapphire eyes.

"You'd really do that?" He replied.

"Yes."

"The agency will have to have a change of name. How about 'Narrow Eye Investigations'?" Blake suggested.

Patricia smiled, surprised, "My old agency name? Not Blue Circle?"

He shook his head, "No. That name died with Darren Maitland." – stepping away, Blake grabbed a chair from near the wall, and brought it over to sit down the other side of the desk, "You know when David and I talked about partnering up, I was apprehensive, but looking back it was probably the making of me. I paid the loan off last year. The place has been a big success. Guess this sort of thing was just what Miami needed."

Patricia brought the file back in front of her and opened it.

Origin

"It's decided then. So, onto the business at hand … these twelve women, they were trying to bring something into our world. I don't think what they ended up resurrecting, was how they had intended it to go." Patricia said.

Blake frowned, "What you mean? They brought Lisa back. That much became more and more obvious to me as it all played out, starting with the discovery of that 'Darren & Lisa forever' message at the hotel."

He briefly recalled how Patricia and himself moved an L-shaped sofa aside at the scene, revealing the blood-written words.

"It certainly looked that way, but I don't think that was their intention. Looking into 'The Sect of the Fallen Angel', they worship some demonic deity, known as 'Nefalym'."

"Nefa-what?"

Patricia passed Blake an illustration on a sheet of paper. It depicted a half-human, half-goat looking creature, with large protruding horns on its head and hoofed feet. It was the same creature that formed the organisation's logo.

"This is some biblical, fire and brimstone shit." He remarked, taking the paper and looking at the illustration.

"Whatever Sarah became, I'd hazard a guess it was half her and half whatever that is."

Blake shuddered, then placed the paper on the desk, laying it face down to stop him looking at it.

"You could be onto something."

Patricia focused on his face, her expression serious, "Nobody is looking into these people Blake. We can't let something like that ever start up again."

"So where do you suggest we begin?"

Patricia looked down at the file again and pulled out a booklet. It had an address of a Church, located in the city.

"A visit to this place could be a start." She said, turning the booklet around and pushed it over to Blake.

He just stared at it apprehensively.

"If like you say, those women were linked to this organisation, we gotta tread carefully. They're clearly into some fucked up shit."

"We will, I've got some ideas." Patricia replied as Blake focused on the photo of a fairly ordinary looking three-story building.

Around half an hour later, both Patricia and Blake were standing outside the same building. Blake's Honda HR-V was parked on the road directly behind them.

"This is the place according to the address. Doesn't look like a satanic cult." Blake remarked.

"Yeah, where's the six-foot standee of Beelzebub? Nah, this looks more like a hostel." Patricia added, stepping towards the door and tried the handle. It was locked but an intercom was fixed to the wall. She glanced to Blake before pressing the button.

After a moment, the intercom's speaker crackled, until a voice was heard.

"Hello?"

"Oh hi, er, is this The Sect of the Fallen Angel?" Patricia asked, leaning close to the intercom.

Blake noticed a security camera up high, a blinking red light on the side as it turned and looked down at them.

Origin

"Who may I ask is enquiring?" The voice replied.

"We're from the university. We're doing a paper on alternative religions. May we come in?"

A brief silence came and went, then a buzzer was heard, and Patricia tried the handle again. The door clicked open, and Patricia ventured inside as Blake followed.

Soon they were seated in an office with dark red wallpaper and a number of strange and creepy images displayed on the walls. Behind a desk sat a bearded man in a black suit and black silk shirt. He had gold rings on the fingers of one hand. The image he presented was eye-catching if not entirely unexpected.

"So erm, what university did you say the two of you were from?" The man asked, inquisitive.

Blake glanced to Patricia, noticing how she was taking the lead with things.

"Florida State. We're tutors in religious studies there." She answered quickly, playing from an internal script she'd conjured up the night before.

Patricia had the kind of looks and charm to convince even the most cynical of audiences. By the way this man was staring at her, she was having the desired effect.

"I see. Well, how may I be of help?"

Blake chose to intervene, "A number of months ago, news broke of a terrible incident involving the deaths of twelve women."

"Oh yes. Awful business. Just awful."

"It was later released to the press that one of the women, an Imelda Drake, had formerly been a member of this very congregation, and rumoured to have held a high position."

The man looked at Blake inquisitively, "I'm not sure what you're implying Mr…"

"Professor… Davies."

"Professor Davies. Every organisation can have some bad seeds, I mean… just look at the Catholic Church."

"Oh, don't get us wrong, we're not implying anything." Patricia then piped up, "We're just after a little information relating to the kind of teachings and the like that are passed onto your members and any opinion you might have as to why someone may go onto commit the kind of crimes as we just referenced."

"On a political standpoint, Miss…"

"Kerrigan."

"Miss Kerrigan, ah, interesting surname. We er, offer the world as we see it, a different path. There is a great deal of corruption in our government, certain religious faiths and that goes as far as The White House. Social media has been a breeding ground for terrorism and school shootings. We believe our teachings offer some hope in an increasingly hopeless society. I wouldn't leap to too many conclusions regarding the imagery you see, a lot of it is simply misunderstood or taken out of context."

"But Satanism, isn't that you know, evil and all that?" Blake asked.

"If you wish to believe the Old Testament. Then again, the Old Testament had issues with homosexuality, amongst

Origin

other lifestyles. I'd like to think the world has come a long way since then."

Blake sat back in his chair. He had to admit, the man had a point. He looked around the room then noticed a rather impressive looking dagger hanging on the wall.

"Nice knife." He remarked.

The man stared at Blake sternly, then looked over his shoulder to it.

"Oh that, yes… afraid it's not the original."

Patricia looked at it also.

"Oh? Looks impressive. So, who has the original?" Blake continued.

"Well, that remains a bit of a mystery. It was last rumoured to be somewhere in New York, but nobody has heard anything about it in years."

"Fascinating. What's it called?"

The man paused, as if uncomfortable with the subject, "Erm, well, it goes by many names, but the one I personally favour is 'The dagger of Hades'. Legend says, it's the only item that can resurrect our Lord." - he pointed to one framed photo depicting the hoofed creature.

"Nefalym?" Patricia remarked.

The man returned his attention to her, sporting an expression like she'd just insulted him. He then forced a smile, before leaning closer.

"Someone's done their homework. However, between you and I, it's all hocus pocus bullshit, but our followers enjoy that kinda thing. I'm more about offering a different viewpoint than confusing people with tales of monsters and boogeymen."

Patricia was finding the man quite engaging even if she was still on the fence about his beliefs. She looked to Blake.

"I see. Well, I'd say that gives us plenty to start with. Thank you Mr…"

"Black, Lucas Black."

"Of course." Blake added then got up, shaking the man's hand as Patricia in turn did the same.

"Nice meeting you. Give my regards to the Dean." Lucas Black then said, staring at Patricia as if he was trying to say something without saying it.

Slightly uneasy, she returned a smile.

Origin

7

Manhattan

Harry and Blake sit in Harry's Volvo Estate outside the imposing, One Police Plaza building of the New York Police Department. Droplets of rain drum against the windscreen as Blake observes Police squad cars exit and enter. Seeing them causes his thoughts to jump back to his former years, back when he was a cop. Good and bad times, but they had still taught him a great deal.

"I think I'll sit this one out, Harry. I can't run the risk of being recognised. There's probably still a file open on me, I mean 'Darren Maitland' in the deep recesses of this place."

Harry glances to him, "That might be wise. I'll just catch up with my contact in the S.I.D and be right back. Shouldn't take too long."

With that he opens the driver's side and climbs out. Blake can't help but jolt as the door slams on Harry's exit. He sighs, feeling uneasy for a variety of reasons.

As he watches Harry disappear through the gates, Blake spots two female officers as they exit, chatting with each other and pass the car. The one officer has shoulder-length curly blonde hair and instantly reminds him of someone. He realises just as quick that it's not who she reminds him of, but the resemblance is uncanny.

Years back

It was late winter. Snow had fallen heavy that year and the TV, shops and streets were giddy with Christmas spirit. Darren Maitland, long before he was Blake, was not a fan of the yuletide build up, felt it was way too over-emphasised and started too soon. Damn, when had it kicked off this year, October? Ridiculous. Back then, Darren was married, had been for about five years, but well, he was also seeing a colleague on the side, a young twenty-something officer named Cassandra. He'd just finished a late shift, nothing all that eventful other than sitting behind a desk all evening, completing paperwork, but he had arranged to meet up with Cassandra at their usual place; a motel on the outskirts of Battery Park.

Arriving in the fairly sparse car park of the establishment, he parked up as his headlights illuminated a row of motel rooms. Light snowfall danced in the glow until he shut off the engine. Darren then noticed a light burning in one window, and as he looked two spaces down, Cassandra's

Origin

distinctive pink Toyota Yaris was parked. *She's already here*, Darren thought as he popped open a glove compartment, fishing around the interior, before retrieving a three-pack of condoms. He briefly glanced to his reflection in the rear-view mirror, like he was expecting a look of disapproval, then opened his door. His hair was a short, brown crew cut, and he was slightly unshaven.

Reaching the motel room door, he went to knock just as the door opened, and he was presented with the gorgeous sight of Cassandra. She was wearing a skimpy gown, undone a little way to show off a voluptuous cleavage. Her blonde hair hung loose down to her shoulders, and she had plenty of makeup on, thick lips painted a rubescent red. Darren smiled, any nerves or pangs of guilt vanishing as she reached forward, forcefully snatched the collar of his jacket, then pulled him inside.

In seconds, Cassandra was undressing Darren, tearing open his Police shirt and pulling his jacket down until his arms were restricted from movement. He was at her mercy, and the growing pressure in his pants proved it was one of a number of things he liked about her. She pushed him onto the bed, a single lamp's glow bathing the surface and he squinted as she proceeded to unbuckle his trousers, tugging them down along with his boxers, until his semi-erect penis was exposed before her face.

"You bring anything?" She asked.

"Right, inside pocket." Darren replied.

Cassandra delved a hand inside his jacket, routing around which was slightly ticklish. She then retrieved the strip of condoms, tearing one open and quickly applied it to his penis.

Wrapping her lips around the head, she rolled back the latex birth control with her mouth, feeling him grow and stiffen in the process.

Soon she had discarded her knickers and was squatting over him, guiding his hardness to her opening, and with a gasp she sank down, burying him to the hilt. Still unable to touch her due to his rolled down jacket sleeves, she proceeded to take from him exactly what she needed, and he loved every glorious second.

Afterwards, Darren lay on his back as Cassandra draped her naked form against him, one leg brushing his thigh, her foot stroking his shin. The sex was always good. They had first got together about six months ago, following a night out with some of the other guys from work. He had offered a lift home and, in hindsight it had been the alcohol she'd consumed, but she came onto him. Darren and his wife 'Eleanor' had been going through a rough patch, a result of IVF treatment that hadn't been working out, following the discovery they were unable to conceive naturally. That and the stresses from work due to a particularly unpleasant case, meant that he and Cassandra ended up fucking right there in the car. After that, they'd chosen to keep it going, even if of late, each encounter had become more of a habit than anything with particular meaning. Either way, it seemed to suit both their needs.

"I better be going." He said quietly.

Cassandra moaned a response, her head against his chest which raised and lowered with his breathing, his heart beating a steady rhythm. They were both wallowing in the warmth of

Origin

each other's bodies, reluctant to move, but one of them at least had a significant other likely wondering where they were.

Darren owned a house located in Brooklyn and it was gone ten by the time he came in through the front door. The small, three-bedroom house was quiet, which immediately put him on edge as he closed the door and removed his over coat.

"Honey?" He called.

More silence. Darren hung his jacket on a hook where another coat with a fur collar hung, showing that Eleanor wasn't out, at least not in the coat she'd had on that morning when she left for work.

Proceeding into the living room, the TV was off and the drapes drawn. Looking around, he then spotted a mug of coffee on a table beside the sofa. He approached, picking it up and found it to be lukewarm.

Returning to the hallway, he went to climb the staircase until he spotted Eleanor standing at the top. She was a pretty brunette of average height, and she was wearing a dressing gown.

"Darren. Where have you been?" She asked accusingly.

Darren just stared at her. He had prepared a suitable story.

"Oh, you know how it is hun, long day on the job. A few of the guys wanted to go for some beers."

He went to ascend and brush past her until he heard a melody playing. *Was that…* he thought suddenly, *no, she wouldn't call him at home.*

Eleanor then held up her cell phone as they stood together at the top of the stairs.

"Think you better answer that, sweetie." She said.

Darren took out an old Nokia burner phone from within his jacket and looked at the screen. It said: 'unknown caller'.

Eleanor waved her cell at him.

"Think I wouldn't find out? Why have you got two phones you son-of-a-bitch?!"

Eleanor had the number to his second phone, the phone he only used for Cassandra.

"Now relax, it's not what it looks like."

Eleanor ended the call.

"You know, I was tempted to ring earlier, but I needed to see the look on your face!" - Eleanor then stormed away along the upstairs hallway and hurried into the master bedroom.

Darren, flummoxed, followed after her. Inside the master bedroom, Eleanor approached a wardrobe, removing her dressing gown to reveal she wore a coral satin slip beneath. She pulled open a drawer and grabbed some clothing, starting to dress.

"What are you doing?" Darren enquired.

"I'm going to my mothers."

"Now hang on, let's talk about this!"

Eleanor, having pulled on a pair of jeans and a sweater over her slip, grabbed a suitcase, placing it on the double bed. A single lamp bathed where the covers were pulled back, like she'd recently vacated it. She started to throw more clothing into the case; underwear, socks, a pair of sneakers, various tops until Darren walked over and grabbed her by her arm. They stared into each other's eyes, and he noticed the pain

Origin

evident in hers. It was a look he had hoped he would never see.

"Hey, just wait, let me explain." He said calmly.

He saw tears appear in her eyelids, threatening to spill over.

"So, who's Cassandra?" She asked.

Darren paused, realising he'd put her name as a contact on the burner. A dumb move in hindsight.

"How'd you find the phone?"

"You probably shouldn't leave it in your pants when I'm doing laundry. I found it the other day. Now, answer my question!"

Her pain was turning to anger.

"Ok. She's er… just a colleague. It means nothing. I… I love you, Eleanor." - he ran his hands up both her arms affectionately.

"How long?"

"What?"

"How long has it been going on? How long you been fuckin' her?"

Darren knew that any answer would be the wrong answer. He turned away, sitting down on the end of the bed as Eleanor just stared, awaiting a response.

"It's pointless going into it. Things haven't been easy for us of late, you must realise that. The IVF, my work…"

"Oh don't give me that! It's my body that's been wrecked! See me going and jumping on the first dick I see? No. You're pathetic, you know that?"

Darren sighed, unable to disagree as he felt tears in his eyes and his emotions overwhelmed him.

66

Eleanor stuffed a few more clothes into the case before running a zip around the edge, taking it from the bed and approached the door. Darren, tears running down his cheeks looked to her then got up, hurrying after her as she left the room.

"El… please, you don't have to go. Let's talk about this. I'm sorry. It will never happen again!" He went to grab her, but she pulled away, marching down the hall.

He followed after her, sobbing.

"You disgust me, Darren. You're an embarrassment of a husband. I'm going to my mothers. We'll talk about this when I've calmed down."

Eleanor then began to descend the staircase, and Darren paused at the top watching her go. He was crying, sniffing up a runny nose.

"Eleanor… I love you." He shouted, as he watched his wife leave the house, slamming the door behind her.

Origin

8

Harry returns to his Volvo and opens the rear hatch. Blake observes him via the car's rear-view mirror as Harry places a large box inside before walking around to the driver's side and climbing in.

"Sorry, took longer than expected." Harry remarks, "I'm retired, but the guys still act like I'm their Lieutenant. Doesn't help that dumb-ass Bryson who replaced me, hasn't the faintest idea how to run a department."

"Did you find anything?"

"Yeah. Some old case files. Not really that much in storage it turns out, but I managed to persuade an old friend in records to let me take some stuff away, for old times' sake."

Blake then ducks down slightly as a Police squad car rolls by the Volvo.

"Let's just get out of here, then." He says nervously.

As the car pulls away from the One Police Plaza building - across the road, a black BMW is parked. A large, heavy-set dark-skinned man is at the wheel, the windows of the car tinted so any passers by would be unable to see inside. He watches the Volvo pull into traffic, waits until another two cars drive by, then fires up the engine and follows.

Eventually, Harry places the large cardboard box on a coffee table. Seated on the sofa at Harry's apartment, Blake looks at the box apprehensively. As much as he may yearn to know more and piece together exactly what happened, what he could discover still fills him with dread.

"What you waiting for?" Harry asks, standing by the table.

The smell of tobacco fills the room as he lights up a cigar. With a sigh, Blake reaches forward and lifts the lid from the box to reveal an assortment of documents and several items in transparent plastic bags. Placing the lid aside, Blake begins to fumble through the contents. Harry watches him with interest as clouds of smoke leave his mouth, the cigar loose between his lips.

Blake removes some crime scene photos, depicting a blonde girl, a messy apartment and a cabinet made up like an altar, complete with lit candles and a five-pointed star on a wall above. He holds the photo of the blonde for Harry to see.

"Tina Lawson." Harry remarks with grim recognition, "A hooker who worked the same block as Lisa Watts. She was found at Joseph's apartment if I recall, along with the body

Origin

of his girlfriend. They were the first of the 'ritualistic' murders."

"Joseph was discovered unconscious, later found to be in a coma." Blake adds, "He died in hospital reportedly the same time Lisa died. It was strange, as if the two of them had some sort of psychic connection." - the memory of the case gradually causes his pulse to race as beads of sweat form on his neck and forehead.

He places the photos on the table, delving back into the box again. Blake then frowns as he clasps his fingers around something rigid. Carefully pulling his hand out, he withdraws a large gem-encrusted, golden dagger.

Harry's eyes widen in amazement.

"Oh my God... I've seen this before!" Blake remarks.

Briefly a memory flashes in his head of the same dagger displayed on a wall. He looks to his right at Patricia Willis.

Harry reaches down as Blake passes him the dagger, "Damn, I think this was found back when we were called to the Watts apartment." He remarks, "If I'm right, it was kind of a talking point at the time, but nothing came of it. I guess it got dumped into evidence and has been there, gathering dust ever since."

"What did that guy call it now? The dagger of hell... no, The dagger of Hades!" Blake exclaims.

Harry turns the weighty dagger over in his hands, admiring the multi-coloured gems imbedded in the handle, the curved, engraved blade glinting.

"I'll fire up the laptop and see if there's any information online."

"Patricia and I met with… with a guy. We er… found out about a religious organisation, a Satanic outfit calling themselves 'Sect of the Fallen Angel'. I er, forget the man's name but, but he was kind of dismissive of the imagery, mysticism etc. He made out it was just bullshit to dress up a political agenda."

Harry nods as he walks away, and as he disappears into another room, Blake picks up the Polaroid of the blonde girl, noticing what appears to be a five-pointed star painted on her exposed upper body.

Outside the brownstone building in Greenwich Village, the Black BMW is parked. The dark-skinned man in the front speaks on a cell phone.

"No problem, I'll keep a close watch on our inquisitive friend, don't you worry now." He says, a hint of Spanish to his accent.

Blake enters an office inside the apartment where Harry is sitting before a laptop. The drapes are partially closed, and the laptop's screen lights up Harry's wrinkled features. His cigar burns in an ashtray beside the laptop, causing strings of smoke to snake into the air.

"Anything?"

"Dagger of Hades is just one of a number of names, another being 'The blade of Oscuridad'. Says here that it originates from Spain. I'd get that thing put in a protective bag or something, 'cause apparently it's over five hundred years old." Harry then details.

Origin

"No way." Blake remarks, shocked.

"I know a guy who is into this occult stuff. Maybe I should give him a call, get a handle on exactly what we're dealing with."

Blake looks at the images on the webpage; crude wall drawings on ancient ruins depicting the hoofed demon on a hilltop, below a red circle (a moon or sun?), the dagger held aloft over a sea of corpses.

*

"We sure this is the place?" Blake asks as he and Harry make their way through an outdoor market area as evening draws in.

"My guy has got a store here. Lots of geeky crap, but trust me when I say, he knows his stuff." Harry replies, holding a steaming plastic coffee cup as he makes his way through the mass of pedestrians.

Blake looks to various stall fronts, selling homemade linen, fresh food, ornaments and other such things. Under different circumstances he'd be interested in browsing, and for sure Patricia would love such a place. However, he wasn't here to pick up a vase that might fetch a good price at auction, he was here for answers.

Soon they reach one such stall, which resembles a comic book shop, posters of Iron Man, Batman along with video game characters adorn makeshift walls. Behind a display of comic books and collectible figurines, sits an overweight, middle-aged man with a thick, untidy beard, wearing a 'Punisher' skull logo t-shirt.

"Lieutenant Benning!" The man says in recognition, placing a graphic novel called 'Watchmen' aside, before offering a chubby hand.

Harry places his coffee on the counter, then takes the man's hand, shaking it firmly.

"Sammy! Good to see you, although it's just Harry these days. I'm retired."

Sammy briefly glances to Blake before refocusing on Harry with a smile.

"Hey, good for you. So, you said you had something for me to look at?"

Blake steps forward removing a satchel from over his shoulder and opens the top flap. Sammy's eyes then widen as Blake produces the dagger. This time it's housed in a transparent bag. Instantly he turns to an iPad propped up on the counter behind the comic books.

"No no no… this can't be. Let me see that." He remarks, one hand tapping the screen of the iPad, the other held out in Blake's direction.

Blake places the bag with the dagger in Sammy's hand.

A short distance from the stall, amongst the crowd of people, stands the dark-skinned man. He handles an antique looking candle stick holder as he subtly looks over, watching the fat guy handle the dagger with interest whilst talking to the two men.

Origin

"You realise what this is, right?" Sammy continues, bringing up a website similar to that which Harry found.

"The blade of Oscuridad. Foretold in ancient texts to be the bringer of eternal darkness. First discovered in a small, mountain settlement in Navarra, Spain. Damn, where'd you find this?"

"Afraid that's classified, Sammy." Harry pipes up.

Sammy admires the dagger, holding the bag up and focusing on it.

"Well, whatever hole you dug this out of, I'd recommend putting it right back. I know you probably think this sort of stuff is just superstition, but I don't know. There's some crazy shit in this world, and we don't really understand it all. I'd air on the side of caution with this one."

He passes the bag back.

"So, it's the real deal, not a fake?" Blake asks.

"The engravings are faded enough to suggest it's age and those stones, they look genuine to me. Going by the weight also, yeah I'd say that thing's real alright."

In the distance, the dark-skinned man watches as the older man shakes the nerdy fat guy's hand, before departing the store with the guy with the blonde mullet. He then raises a cell phone and starts to type out a text:

'You're not going to believe what I've just seen. Our search may finally be over.'

He attaches a zoomed-in photo he's taken of Blake passing the bag containing the dagger to Sammy. He then sends the text, moving from the stall, and continues to follow Harry and Blake.

Origin

9

Miami

Patricia eased the door open to Blake's office at the agency. In the outer office, various other agents were leaving, pulling on coats and chatting amongst themselves.

"Come on Blake, we're heading out now."

Blake looked up from a desk partially illuminated by the glow of a small desk lamp, the rest of the office in darkness. He had been studying some of the merchandise Patricia had gathered detailing the sect, gradually developing a headache as a result.

"I don't think I'm in the right mood. This place, it was a dead end. Where do we realistically go from here?" He asked, looking over to Patricia as she walked inside, coming to stand before Blake's desk.

She placed her hands on the surface, peering at him with those kind eyes of hers.

"Listen. You have been through a lot. We both have. But you also need to recognise when it's time to take a step back. This has been arranged for you, but also for the agency. A new beginning. So, get your ass into gear and switch off from all of this, at least for one night."

Blake smiled, tidying the flyers and booklets into a filing tray that already overflowed with similar items, then got up, grabbing his jacket as Patricia responded with a wide, child-like grin.

Patricia clinked glasses with Anna, the young black girl, as Blake ordered a pint, standing at a bar with two of the guys. The establishment they had chosen had a touristy, tropical theme, complete with wicker furnishings and fake indoor palm trees. The heavy-set Hawaiian barman was handsome, and the vibe was pleasant enough to push recent events to the back of the mind.

"Not having something stronger, Patricia?" Anna asked as she herself handled a rum topped off with coke.

"Maybe later. I er… I just want to keep a level head, you know, for Blake." Patricia answered, not exactly ready to tell the world her 'news' just yet - after all, she had barely come to terms with it herself.

She eyed Blake as he lifted his pint to his lips, gulping it down. He sure needed this, she mused, more than anyone.

Origin

As gentle music played from a band on a nearby stage, the members of the agency had convened to a table within a more private area away from the noise of the other patrons.

"So… if I can have everyone's attention. I'd just like to say a few words." Blake said, as the chatting gradually ceased amongst his co-workers.

Patricia lingered beside Anna and a few others in the background.

"This has been a very troubling time for the agency, as you're all aware but, I think I speak for everyone here in saying, we've overcome and are still standing, prepared to face whatever this crazy world might throw our way."

Heckled words of agreement rang out, along with some brief clapping.

"After what happened to David," Blake continued, "I'd also like to make a toast. So, if I could ask everyone to raise your glasses."

Patricia raised her tonic water as the others did the same with their chosen drinks.

"David. You were both a mentor and a valued friend. I'll miss you, buddy. Everyone, to David!"

"To David!" was returned in chorus.

Each person drank. Blake finished his pint, placing the glass triumphantly on the table, then Patricia joined him as he put an arm around her waist; much to her, and everyone else's surprise.

"Patricia here has been my backbone ever since she decided to join us here in the sunshine state. Therefore, I am happy to announce that she'll be taking over David's share of the business. That being said, there is also going to be a name change to reflect Patricia's involvement."

Mumbled voices passed through the group like bees buzzing around a rose bush, faces looking to Patricia with suspicion. She blushed, not used to having so many eyes looking in her direction.

"Yes, er, thank you Blake." She responded, "I'm so honoured to be a part of this agency."

Blake squeezed her affectionately against him - a little too affectionate for her comfort levels.

"Nonsense, the honour is all ours. And so, from Monday, H&T will henceforth be officially known as 'Narrow Eye Investigations'."

After more mumbled words, several claps began that soon developed into applause. Glasses clinked and Patricia separated from Blake as the other agents hugged and kissed her. Their response to an announcement she herself had been apprehensive about, now filled her with a happiness she thought she might never feel again.

As the hours added up, and it was approaching 10:30p.m. Patricia stepped out of a side entrance to the bar, in desperate need of some air. She had never been that much for socialising but had wanted to do something special for Blake, set him back on track, back to who he was. As a warm breeze caressed her face, she reached into her handbag as it hung from a strap over her shoulder and retrieved her cell phone. She checked her messages as she stood under the glow of the bar's flickering neon sign, a duo of moths buzzing around it and bouncing off the light. She had sent a couple of texts to

Origin

Malcolm, her brother but was yet to receive a response. She prayed he was ok, even if the regret she felt for leaving after the trouble he'd got himself into, still stung. However, she had been assured Malcolm would be fine, so hoped that someday soon, she'd get to tell him he was going to be an uncle.

A high-pitched clatter then interrupted the quiet of the night, and she lowered her phone to look down the side alley she was standing in. The area ahead was almost pitch black. As she stepped out from the glow of the sign, she looked again to see a man emerge from the shadows. She instantly recognised him as Lucas Black. Her pulse quickened in reaction.

"Miss Kerrigan? Or should I say, Miss Willis?" He announced, wearing the same black suit and matching shirt.

"What are you doing here?" Patricia responded.

"I was quite fascinated why someone would be asking about my business. Then when I did a little digging and found you came to me under false pretense, well, I was disappointed."

"Hey, I don't want any trouble. Blake and I…" Patricia stammered, nerves turning to fear.

"I know you're P.I.'s Miss Willis. I can't really have you looking into our affairs. So unfortunately, I'm going to have to send a message."

Before Patricia could say anything further, she was grabbed from behind, a hand clamped over her mouth to muffle her cries as her arm was pushed painfully behind her back. Her eyes bulged in terror as Lucas Black approached, slipping his hands one at a time into a pair of leather gloves.

A short while later, Blake stumbled out of the front of the bar along with a few of the others. He had clearly had a few beers and going by the pulsing dizziness in his head, it was time to head home. He glanced around himself as he staggered drunkenly, then turned to one of the guys.

"Thought Patricia was out here." He remarked and stumbled slightly before wandering into the side alley.

As he proceeded, swaying from side to side, vision jittery like a TV that needed tuning, his foot made contact with a discarded soda can, which rolled away into the shadowy dark of the alley. A faint moaning then reached his ears…

Proceeding alongside a dumpster, Blake froze in mid-stride upon discovering two long legs, the one foot bare. A high heeled shoe lay discarded a short distance away. The moaning had become clearer. A terrible feeling gushed through his body and he stepped forward to peer beyond the dumpster, and to his horror, discovered Patricia lying awkwardly and looking barely conscious. Her face was bruised and covered in blood; part of her suit torn.

"Oh God, no… Patricia!" He exclaimed, dropping to his knees and leaned over her.

He touched the side of her head, cradling it as he lifted her slightly. She'd obviously been attacked. As he felt his heart pound his chest, he lay her back down, then shot a look back to the alley.

Origin

"Someone call 911!! We need an ambulance here!!" He yelled as panic took over.

A couple of the others appeared at the entrance to the alley. Anna then retrieved her cell, looking concerned and quickly began to tap numbers. Blake, trembling, looked back to Patricia who continued to moan in agony, and he took hold of her hand, struggling to keep his emotions at bay.

10

As it approached midnight, Blake paced up and down a hospital corridor. He was struggling to rationalise how this could have happened. She had been right there, enjoying herself and in her condition, hadn't even been drinking. Patricia was being sensible. Who would do this?

The door of a hospital room then opened, and a male Asian doctor emerged.

"Doc. Er… how is she?" Blake asked, rushing over.

"Are you…"

"A friend. We work together. I er… I was the one who found her."

"Well, she's stable. As you're not a relative, we can't divulge details, but she's been hurt rather badly I'm afraid. We discovered some swelling around the brain. You

Origin

understand with this sort of assault, we automatically have to inform the Police."

Blake nodded, not really caring about anything other than Patricia's wellbeing.

"Can I see her?"

The doctor smiled, "I don't see why not. Although she's been slipping in and out of consciousness."

Blake hurried past the doctor and entered the room to see a heart monitor bleeping. As Blake reached the bedside, with a heavy heart he observed Patricia lying with her eyes closed, a bandage around her head, face awash with purple & blue bruises, and a horrific swelling around one eye.

He took a seat in a chair beside the bed and reached for her hand, taking hold as an I.V drip hung from the wrist. His emotions overwhelmed him as he brought her hand to his face, laying a kiss on her knuckles as the tears flowed. After a moment, he heard a groan and slowly looked to her to discover Patricia's eyes slightly open.

"Hey…" Blake responded.

"W-Where am I?" Patricia replied weakly.

"You're in hospital. You were, erm… attacked."

Patricia winced, clearly in pain.

"They… they told me… to stay away." She then said.

Blake stood up, leaning over her to listen.

"Who? Who did this? Tell me Patricia. Who did this to you?"

"Black… it was… Lucas Black."

"That fuckin' guy from this morning?"

84

Patricia closed her eyes. It was taking all her strength just to speak.

"This was a warning, Blake. Next time they'll kill me, or you."

Blake couldn't think straight. In that moment, he wanted to track down who had done this and feed them their own intestines... yet also realised Patricia was being deadly serious.

"Just focus on getting better. That's all that matters now."

Patricia groaned her response.

Minutes later, Blake walked down the outer corridor. The thoughts racing through his head disturbed him. Violent thoughts mixed with the images of his fiancé Sarah... that face, those glowing yellow eyes, the jagged teeth, seconds before he pulled the trigger on a twelve gage.

"You've done it again." a whispered, female voice then said, catching him off guard and caused him to stand still.

"What do you mean?" He answered.

"Everyone you care about. They always get hurt. Now Patricia. She trusted you. You brought her here, to Miami. And now she is clinging to life in a hospital bed. It's all your fault. She could have died."

"That's not true."

"Oh isn't it, Blake? Look what happened to me. You killed me and it's only a matter of time before you kill Patricia too. Why don't you do us all a favour and..." - then Sarah whispered directly into his ear, standing behind him, "kill yourself!"

Origin

"Get away! Get out of my head!" Blake shouted, putting both hands over his ears as he staggered down the corridor, "You're not fuckin 'real!!"

A passing nurse froze in response to his outburst and looked over to him, "Sir? Is everything alright?"

Blake rested against the wall, panting and began to calm himself. He didn't look at the nurse.

"Yeah… it's … it's fine."

The nurse proceeded on her way as Blake walked in the opposite direction. He then became aware of distant laughter. Looking down the remainder of the long white corridor, he watched as ahead of him, the naked, hoofed Sarah wandered out from a doorway. Puppeteer strings seemingly supported her from above, creating wobbly and awkward movement. Her long, white hair hung down to her waist. He focused on her as he paused again. She then turned, looking directly at him and, as she did so… her face metamorphosed into someone else… that once brilliant white hair turning jet black. It was Lisa. She looked at Blake with an innocent expression and he focused on her, shocked, just as a *thump-thump-thump* noise alerted him.

Blake turns and finds himself in his bedroom at Harry's apartment – in New York.

"Blake?" comes Harry's voice, "You up? I've made some coffee."

Struggling to shake the thoughts, the memories from his head, he runs the zip up the front of his over coat and grabs his wallet from a chest of drawers before approaching the door.

In the outer hallway, Harry, wearing a dressing gown, holds a mug of coffee in one hand. As the bedroom door opens, he notices Blake is already dressed.

"Oh. You off out?" He asks.

"Yeah, I er… I need to get to the cemetery. I've put this off long enough." He replies and brushes past Harry, ignoring the hot beverage.

"Want me to drop you off?"

"No, thank you but, I'll get a cab. I just need some time alone, to think." Blake responds as Harry watches him head for the front door, open it then leave.

Green-Wood Cemetery
Brooklyn

About an hour later, Blake kneels at Lisa's grave, a looming, graffiti-defaced headstone before him, casting its shadow as the early morning sun bleeds through the overhanging trees. Tears sting his eyes.

"Here I am Lisa. It's only taken seven years. I… I had this whole speech prepared, about you being my salvation and me condemning you to some unholy fate. Yet really, I'm here for answers. I know now you'll never rest, not whilst I breathe air. Not whilst there's people in my life I care about. So I guess I'm hoping you'll let me know in some way, what it is I need to do now, to finish this once and for all."

Origin

Glancing to an adjacent grave a metre or so away, he notices a name on an even more graffiti-defaced headstone: 'J Watts' - *perhaps Joseph, Lisa's younger brother?* He wonders.

Returning his attention to Lisa's headstone, he reads her name, eyes falling to her date of birth. To his surprise, it would have been her birthday. April 25th - today. If his estimation is right, she'd have been about 29. Damn, same age as Patricia.

With feelings of guilt and regret taking control, he wipes his eyes on the sleeve of his coat before turning and grabbing his satchel. Placing it on the slightly overgrown grave, he unfastens the straps. Opening the top flap, he delves a hand inside - and removes the dagger. The large, curved blade seems to glow in the sunlight.

"This is the key, isn't it Lisa? Something about this thing, it holds the secret to bringing your spirit some peace. I can feel it! I'm meant to save you! Lay you to rest … and perhaps, free myself at the same time." - he runs a hand over the blade, then winces as the sharp edge catches his skin.

Looking at his open palm, he has cut himself. Not deep, but enough to cause a slither of blood. Cursing to himself, he looks again to the grave before standing up. Something hard then makes impact with the back of his head. Jolting, he goes to react … yet before he can, everything goes black and his legs give way.

Behind, at the foot of Lisa Watts 'grave stands the dark-skinned man, clutching a baton. As he looks down at Blake, lying unconscious, he's joined by Juanita Equarez.

"Just as we suspected. If that's really the genuine article." She remarks, seeing the dagger lying on the dirt beside Blake.

"One way to find out." The dark-skinned man says and reaches down, picking up the dagger.

"You got a photo?" He asks, admiring the golden dagger as he turns it over, laying eyes on the gems and engravings.

Juanita holds up a cell phone showing a photo of the dagger. It looks identical.

"This, Drago, along with the eclipse, has been ordained. It's a sign." She remarks.

Drago looks at her and says, "His time has finally come." - and leans towards Juanita and kisses her long and hard.

Blake remains out cold at their feet. After a moment, Juanita looks down at him.

"What about this guy?" She asks.

"Help me get him to the car. We'll dump him at the river." Drago replies, then slips the dagger into his trench coat, before reaching down and grabbing Blake by the ankles.

Juanita steps aside as he drags Blake from the grave, leaving a smear of blood on the dirt. She then takes Blake's arms and together, they lift and carry him away.

*

Blake opens his eyes, the sound of a flowing stream meets his ears, and he coughs, before rolling onto his back. The ground is moist, and the sun beats down from above, the heat warming his face. Gradually he becomes aware of the throbbing in his head, then slowly sits up to find himself beside a river. For a moment he has to gather his bearings,

Origin

until the sound of a tire scraping dirt alerts him. He looks to his right to see a girl on a push bike, dressed in a hoodie, skinny jeans and sneakers.

"Hey, Mr… you ok?" She asks.

Blake is bewildered. He doesn't know where he is exactly or what has happened.

"Who are you?" He asks with weakness, and scrambles to his feet, standing up to look at the girl on the bike properly.

Her mode of transport resembles a BMX. Recognition hits him as he looks at her face. She's the girl from the brothel.

"Don't I…" He stammers, as she climbs off her bike, letting it drop to the ground and hurries over.

"I was following Juanita. They were watching you, ya know. They have been since 'other day." She says, a tuft of blonde hair peeking out from her hood.

She checks him over, touching the back of his head and he gasps in pain.

"They didn't intend to kill you I don't think, but Mr, you gotta stay away from her and her people. They're dangerous."

Blake stares at her as he holds a hand to the back of his head - there is a definite lump.

"What's your name? Why you helping me?"

"Name's Gemma. I came to New York about a month ago, looking into a few things after my bro went missing."

"I don't follow."

"You're not the only one interested in that Spanish bitch's affairs."

Blake sighs, appreciating the girl's presence. Panic suddenly consumes him. He looks around nervously, until he discovers his satchel lying slightly in the water. Rushing over, he grabs it and pulls open the flap, delving a hand inside as Gemma observes with confusion.

"What ya looking for?" She asks.

"Fuck!" Blake curses, then looks back at her, "I gotta get back to the city. They stole something from me."

"Stole what?"

"Never you mind. I gotta go, er, thanks for your concern, but… I'm ok."

Blake goes to leave, until Gemma hurries over and grabs his arm.

"Listen, Mr… I'll explain. I gotta job at that place to look into Juanita Equarez. I know about her involvement in the certain organisations. I've overheard some stuff. So if that's what you're looking at also, maybe we could help one another."

Blake looks into her hazel-coloured eyes and notices sincerity. He also realises she's much prettier without makeup running down her face - or a dick in her mouth.

"Ok, but I'm not cadging a lift on your bike."

Gemma responds with a smirk.

92

PART TWO

94

1

New York

2008

February

She rolled the soft nylon in her hands, bringing it to the tips of her toes, before carefully applying it to her foot, unfurling the sheer fabric to her ankle and then to her calf, continuing up her leg before stopping at her thigh. An embroidered hem complimented its twin on her neighbouring thigh, the sheer black of the stockings making her legs look toned and incredibly long. Wriggling her toes she admired the effect, before slipping her foot into a high heeled shoe. Reaching down, she fastened a strap securely, before finally standing.

Lisa Watts approached a full-length mirror serenaded by Green Day's 'Wake Me Up When September Ends' playing

Origin

on a radio. Wearing her best lace lingerie, it was like looking at a model and not actually her own reflection, her long black hair cascading from her head to crash at her shoulders. Casting eyes over her body, she still liked how she looked, even if currently, she did not like herself all that much. She was approaching twenty-two but spiritually, felt far older. Life hadn't exactly gone the way she envisioned when she was younger. Part of the reason was her own fault; financial troubles, an on / off drug habit... others a case of circumstance, all of which had led her to where she was today, staying at a friend's crappy apartment and about to probably make the worst mistake of her life. Any alternative however, had so far eluded her.

Stepping out of the apartment door minutes later, wearing a leather jacket over a tight leather skirt and a cheap white blouse, Lisa was met by Tina. Her friend walked up a graffiti strewn corridor, her own high-heeled boots echoing as they clicked on the hard flooring. Lisa had known Tina for a couple of years, and she stood out with her garish red PVC jacket, and had flowing blonde hair that would catch anyone's eye. As the two of them met up they hugged briefly, then Tina focused on her, all serious.

"Hey, relax. It'll be fun, and anyway, what better way to hustle a guy than for the contents of his wallet?"

An apprehensive Lisa just smiled, trying to ignore the growing crop of butterflies nesting in her stomach.

"Let's just get outta here then." She replied with a face that failed to hide her reluctance, and brushed past Tina, proceeding up the corridor.

Craig Micklewright

Tina watched her go, understanding - she had been there. First night jitters... but two year's and over a hundred johns later, she barely thought that deeply anymore... after all, her job kept her in good shoes, the odd piece of jewellery and that miserable landlord off her back.

Meanwhile in one of the other apartments, a man slightly younger than the two women was lying on a bed, a sheet draped over him, thin enough to create the outline of his naked body as he observed a European-looking girl exit a bathroom, lamplight highlighting her equally naked form. She had cropped, pixie-cut brown hair, complimented by a thick triangle of pubic hair at her groin. Reaching the end of the bed, she smirked upon noticing how the sheet was moving between the man's legs, showing that he was touching himself.

"I got an idea, lover… use this on me whilst we fuck." She remarked then held up a leather belt, it's strap swaying as it dangled from her grip, a metal buckle glinting in the lamplight.

The man frowned, failing to catch on. An intricate tribal-looking tattoo covered the upper portion of his right arm and shoulder, his body muscular.

"You wanting me to whip you?" He asked, sitting up and withdrew his hand from beneath the sheets.

On a bedside cabinet sat an ashtray littered with cigarette butts as well as a used needle on a saucer within traces of brown liquid.

"Not quite… I'd like you to choke me… but trust me, it's the ultimate hit."

Origin

She climbed onto the bed, crawling on hands and knees towards him, her strong perfume filling the man's nostrils as she grew nearer. They embraced, the man rolling on top of her, exposing his bare ass. He stared intently into her wide eyes, then gradually began to slide the belt around her neck.

"You're so fuckin' nasty." He said with a grin as he began to tighten the belt, and slowly it constricted against her throat.

"Yes, that's it lover… now, put it in me." She groaned, closing her eyes.

The man kissed her firmly on her thick lips whilst reaching between their bodies to guide his steel-hard erection to her awaiting wetness.

The girl then grunted as he forced his way inside, burying himself to the hilt. Gasping from the sensation of her inner-warmth, he looked at her exotic, smouldering features as her eyes opened slowly and she mirrored his lust-filled gaze. He moved against her, at first gentle, then more demanding, with little need to prolong the moment, just desperate for release.

Lisa walked along the kerb of the sidewalk. The evening had turned out warm for the time of year and it had not yet rained despite what the forecast had promised, which was a blessing. How long was she expected to stay out here? She understood that their pimp, Carlos expected certain earnings each night, but the exact figure escaped her. Whatever the outcome, Lisa just yearned for the sanctity of her bed and the night to be over before it had begun.

In the apartment, the man shunted violently against the girl as she groaned and yelped. His breath bounced off her cheek as he pushed himself closer and closer to release, urging the sensations forward as his rigid penis stung with each impalement. He didn't care if she was enjoying it, tugging on the belt strap as her face grew crimson, the oxygen being squeezed out of her. He continued, the bed rattling and the springs of the mattress joining it with a chorus in time with the man's slapping hips. And as he came, pressing himself firmly against her body, a final tug on the strap sealed his girlfriend's fate.

A car pulled up to the kerb. The window rolled down and Tina gestured Lisa forward.

"Go on girl, you take this one. I'll wait here for the next guy. You be careful now and… try and enjoy yourself."

Lisa looked to the car as a gentle tune spilled out from within, along with a cloud of cigarette smoke. She reached the door then leaned forward, having unbuttoned part of her blouse and as she looked into the interior, a man with short brown hair and a nice smile stared back - at first admiring her cleavage then looking to her face.

"You looking for a good time, Mr?" Lisa rolled off just as Tina had taught her.

The man looked in his mid-thirties and wasn't bad looking. *You never know*, she thought, *I may have struck lucky*.

"Erm… perhaps. Wanna jump in, sweetheart?" He responded.

Lisa glanced back to Tina who returned a smile and a nod of encouragement.

Lisa stood upright and opened the passenger door, climbing in as Tina watched then observed the rest of the

Origin

passing traffic as the car drove away. She too wished the night to be over, even though it had barely begun.

"So, you local Mister?" Lisa asked the man as they sat together in the car.

He had lowered the radio and stubbed out his cigarette. If nothing else, this guy seemed to have manners. She looked to him, noticing how the light from street lamps and neon signs seemed to highlight the subtle whiskers of a goatee. He had a nice jacket on and as a hand gripped the wheel, she noticed what looked like a wedding ring.

"Yeah, here in Springdale." He answered after a pause long enough for Lisa to almost forget her question.

"Oh right. You don't look from 'round here. This is kind of a bad neighbourhood."

A tinge of nerves became evident within herself. *If he was from this part of the city, he surely wasn't as respectable as he appeared*, she pondered.

"It's not that bad and well, it suits my work."

"Oh? What work is that?"

The man leaned over, reaching for the glove compartment before her, opening it to take something from inside. He then produced a business card as the tops of her stockings peeked out from the hem of her skirt.

Lisa took it between self-manicured fingers and read what was stencilled on one side:

'Darren Maitland,

Private Investigator'

100

Craig Micklewright

The man lay on his back, panting as sweat glistened all over his body. *God damn, she was right. That was the fuck of the century.* He slowly reached to the bedside cabinet and retrieved a cigarette stub, reigniting it on a disposable, then took a lingering drag. After a few seconds he became aware that his girlfriend was not moving ... and in fact, he couldn't even hear her breathing. With a jolt of realisation he sat up, the reality of what they had been doing and the clear risks involved hitting him like a sledgehammer to the face. He looked to her - the belt was tight around her throat - too tight. To add to the horrible image, her eyes were bulging and bloodshot. Panic flooded through him like a burst damn and he hurried to unfasten the belt, tugging at it until it slackened in his hands. He then stared at her, hopeless, horrified. His worst fears could not be denied. 'Elizabet' ... was dead.

Origin

2

The man scrambled from the bed. In his heightened panic, he rushed naked into another room then fumbled along the wall for a light switch. Eventually the overhanging bulb came to life, and he was immediately presented with a carefully drawn five-pointed star on the facing wall, above a cabinet made up to look like an altar. Red, unlit candles stood either end in candle stick holders that looked antique. Trying to steady his breathing, his heart beating so fast he could have had a heart attack, the man rushed to the cabinet and inspected the items on display. Jewellery depicting imps and a carved naked woman, tarot cards, incense sticks, a wooden box and finally the item he was looking for - a leather-bound book. Picking it up he hurried his fingers through the pages, then stopped at one with an illustration of some half-man half-goat creature, hovering over a body. The words on the next page were not in English, an ancient language, but it did not matter, this was the passage he needed. He just hoped now that it worked.

Lisa Watts gyrated on Darren Maitland's lap in the driver's seat of his car where it was parked in a back alley, and they kissed passionately. She hadn't been expecting this. She had thought her first time with a client would be awkward, humiliating but there was something about this man. He was gentle, maybe a little sad but she felt as she rode him, like she was bringing him a happiness that had been hopelessly absent from his life, and that made the task all the easier.

Darren's kisses moved from her lips to her neck, then to her breasts. He took a dark brown nipple between his teeth, a gentle bite that ignited her loins and brought her closer. She increased her movements, his rigid phallus rubbing at just the right spot, and she bit her lip as he mouthed her breasts whilst gripping her hips. With an agonising grunt that the two of them gave in unison, an orgasm was unleashed like an animal freed from its cage. The rush combined so perfectly that neither could tell who it originated from - a cocktail of pleasure sending shivers through both their bodies. Just for a moment, they stared at each other, amazed.

The man dragged Elizabet's lifeless body into the middle of the room a few feet from the altar and stood over it, raising a pen knife in one hand as the now lit candles flickered behind. The pentagram on the wall glistened in the subdued light. Running the knife over his other palm, blood seeped out and he held his hand over Elizabet, allowing the blood to drip and create a polka dot pattern across her breasts and

Origin

abdomen. Reaching to the book, lying open at the desired page, the man began to read a passage out loud.

'Obsecro Domine, exaudi vocem meam. Filia tua in tenebras incidit et ideo te supplex peto, da mihi virtutem tuam. Afferte ei iterum calefacies, et spiritum da iterum ut serviat tibi. Obsecro, o tenebrse Domine, da mihi hoc desiderium, et voluntas tua in aeternum ero servus tuus!'

Lisa was sitting in the passenger seat fastening the buttons on her blouse as Darren started the car's engine. The vibration seemed to pulse through her feet and legs. He lit a cigarette then offered her one from a pack of Marlboro, but she declined.

"No. Thank you. I've never smoked and not likely to start now." She said, and pulled out a compact makeup case, flipping it open to check her face. Her lipstick was a touch smeared.

"So, what's your name? You already know mine." Darren asked as he snapped shut his silver zippo before rolling his window down, exhaling smoke into the alley.

The temptation to give a false name was there, but Lisa felt something within herself that told her this man wasn't a threat.

"Lisa." She replied quietly.

"That's a nice name. I… er, suppose I should get your money."

The slightly awkward yet pleasant moment was spoilt by the reminder that she wasn't on a date. She hadn't just got with a guy in a club. The reality was, she had just had sex for money, and the reveal of his wallet was a bitter pill to swallow.

She so wanted to refuse. Heck, she had enjoyed herself, it had been better than she could have anticipated. Carlos however, would have a very different way of looking at it, and the fact she had once nursed a broken nose inflicted on Tina, told Lisa she could not come away empty handed.

Darren took out a wad of bills, folding them and offered them to her. With reluctance she held out her hand, but took the money from him regardless, quick to stuff it inside her jacket.

"That enough? I wasn't sure…"

Lisa nodded without really processing his question. The exchange of cash for 'services rendered' suddenly felt degrading, and she turned to open her door, the need to escape overwhelming.

"Hey, what is it? Lisa? I have more if that's what it is …here." Darren remarked picking up on her change of mood as he delved into his wallet again, the smoke from the cigarette between his lips drifting through the car interior.

"No, please it's fine I just, I have to go now."

Darren grabbed her arm, and she shot a look back at him. Her eyes were wide and on the brink of tears.

"Hey. do you want me to drop you back?" He asked as he took his cigarette and tossed it out the window.

His face was sincere. *This was a good man. She hadn't been foolish thinking so.*

"No, it's ok, it's not far."

"You know, tonight meant something to me." Darren added.

Origin

Lisa blushed slightly, understanding, "I had a nice time too." She replied, the horrible feeling fading as quickly as it had risen.

He then leaned closer, and they kissed, slowly and with an affection that surprised them both. When they parted, they just stared into each other's eyes.

Lisa smiled and turned away, climbing out of the car and closed the door behind her. Darren remained motionless for a few seconds as the scent of perfume lingered and watched her leave, her statuesque form gradually disappearing into the dark. He sighed, hopeful he would stumble upon her again, and with the thought sitting comfortably in his head, he adjusted the gears and reversed away from where he had parked.

The man stood over Elizabet's body … waiting … nervous. The rush of adrenaline had aroused him, and his erection jutted proudly from a shaven groin. A tattoo on his belly read 'leave the gun, take the cannoli' – a quote from The Godfather. In the silence, if an ant crawled by his foot, he was sure he would hear it. And then a hand clasped his shoulder. Jolting, he staggered forward, almost tripping against her legs, and turned to see a figure, engulfed in shadow as the two candles blew out.

"What the fuck?"

He could hear an unsteady breathing like the air was struggling to leave the creature. As he looked, his eyes ran down a cloaked body to the floor, and to his continued unease he discovered hooves.

Craig Micklewright

"Shedding your blood for this... girl." the creature then said, a voice so deep it rattled through the room like a tremor, "Was enough to grab my attention, but I will need more than that to bring her back."

The man just stared, terrified and amazed, "What do you want of me?" He asked.

"A life for a life. At the stroke of midnight, give me a soul and your girlfriend, she might live again."

The creature then stepped back into the darkness and incredibly the candles reignited. As the room was illuminated once more, the man discovered that the creature was gone.

He looked down to Elizabet, then glanced over to a clock on the wall. It was approaching eleven. There was still time.

Tina paced the sidewalk on the street as another car slowed, earning her attention, before driving on. Likely lonely, horny men who's wives didn't understand them or would look disgusted when they brought up the suggestion of getting pee'd on. Tina had seen it all, done it all and she wasn't even thirty. That's what an abortion at fifteen and a healthy addiction to heroine will do for your career prospects once high school just became the thing a girl gets kicked out of.

She thought of Lisa as she walked back and forth, the mildness of the night rapidly transforming into a chilly breeze. She buttoned up her red PVC jacket trying to find a little comfort as the night dragged on and she hadn't even scored one client. Carlos was not going to be happy if she didn't at least get paid for a handjob. He'd expect her to pay

Origin

another way, the way that left bruises and caused her to have the runs for two days straight.

Tina then heard a scrape of a shoe against paving and turned on her heels to be met by the man from the apartment next door to her own. He was wearing a hoodie and sweatpants.

"Joseph? Fuck, you startled me. What you doing out here?"

Joseph didn't respond, staring at her with a weird look to his eyes. *Was he high?* She knew he and Elizabet did drugs, even scored some off of them from time to time.

"What's the matter, cat got ya tongue?"

Still no reply. Tina sighed and turned away.

"Whatever man, I'm working so scram." She said and walked back towards the kerb.

A passing car slowed down as it's headlights briefly lit her up. She looked to the driver who was blatantly checking her out. Then as if alerted by something, he hit the gas and with a screech of tires raced away.

Suddenly Joseph came behind Tina and dug something hard into her ribs. She gasped then looked down and was horrified to see a revolver. She went to pull away, but he grabbed her and spoke quietly into her ear.

"Make a sound and you're dead. Now come with me!"

Tina's eyes bulged and her heart skipped a beat.

"Joseph? What's got into you?" She squirmed.

"Shut up!" He said firmly then pulled her away with him, marching her towards a side street next to the apartment building. All Tina could do was comply.

3

Lisa walked down the street towards the apartment building. Despite what she had said to Darren, the walk turned out longer than she realised, and in the heels she wore, her feet had started to sting. She paused and balanced herself with a hand to a streetlamp, removing one shoe and rubbing the bottom of her stocking-clad foot. Standing upright again she took her shoes off, dangling them from her fingers then continued walking.

A car pulled up beside her. She halted in reaction giving out a sigh. She really wasn't in the mood to get picked up again just yet.

"Move along buster, I'm off duty." She shouted.

"Sucked enough dick for one night, Lisa?" A voice then responded, and she gasped, recognising it and as she turned, she saw her pimp, Carlos at the wheel of a white Jaguar.

Origin

He was a well-built, tanned Spanish man with a bald head, aged in his forties. In the few times they had met, his intimidating presence had unnerved her, tonight being no different.

"Oh… Carlos. Er, I was just taking a break. I'll er… I'll be back to it any minute now."

Carlos revelled in how she trembled and fumbled her words before him.

"Get in the car, honey, I know a corner that might pick up the pace. The night is still young, after all."

Lisa checked a silver wristwatch her Auntie had given her for her eighteenth birthday. It was almost eleven thirty. She approached the passenger side, opened the door and climbed in. As she sat down Carlos clamped a hand on her thigh, several gold rings on his fingers and he stank of too much cologne. She stared at him as he looked her over, leeringly.

"God damn, you're a hot little thing, aren't you?"

She faked appreciation of his compliment, forcing a smile.

"We'll stop off somewhere first. Just a perk of the job, you understand."

Lisa's mouth twisted into a grimace, and she looked away.

Carlos then removed his hand from her thigh as he trod down on the gas, and the jag speeded off down the street.

11:55

Joseph stood in the room where the altar was located. In the background, feint whimpering noises could be heard. Stripped back down to his underwear, nothing more than black briefs, he ran a hand over several items on the altar, before pausing at the wooden box. Slowly he lifted the lid to reveal a large, unique looking dagger on a bed of red velvet. Its golden blade was curved and engraved; the handle encrusted with a variety of gems. According to Elizabet, she had stolen it off a friend a few months back, and as he stood looking at it, Joseph was suddenly overcome with a feeling - he had to use it. He took the dagger in his hand, looking at it admiringly then turned, walking out of the room and stepping over the body of his girlfriend on the way - now covered with a bedsheet.

In the main bedroom, lying awkwardly on the bed was Tina - tied and gagged. Cable ties secured her arms and legs to the four corners of the bed, she had been stripped to just her knickers, and a gag was tied around her head, only allowing for her moans of despair. Drawn messily over her upper body was a resemblance to the pentagram that adorned the wall above the altar.

"You should know, this isn't personal Tina. I like you, but I love my Elizabet. There's no other way for me. You're just collateral damage." He said as she squirmed, eyes bulging, and she tried to struggle in her bonds but to no avail.

Over by a window the leather-bound book sat on a chest of drawers, open at a particular page and Joseph approached

Origin

then checked the clock on the wall again. It was almost midnight. He glanced back to a terrified Tina once more, then reached down to the book, failing to notice how a breeze from the open window turned the page. Picking up the book, he re-approached the bed.

"I promise, it will be quick." He said as he climbed onto the mattress, kneeling upright beside Tina as she visibly trembled and breathed heavily.

He raised the book and began to read the passage displayed on the page - *the wrong page*. His words once again recited an ancient language.

01:25

Lisa opened her eyes. She could smell the pungent smell of spilt semen in the air. She couldn't believe how her night had spiralled from what had seemed such a tender and surprising start. Lying face down on a sofa bed, only partially clothed, she raised her head slowly, her breasts crushed beneath her weight until she lifted herself up on her arms. Looking down, drool and a little bit of blood stained a cushion. She ached from over use, orifices feeling stretched, torn, possibly ruined. Carlos had taken a detour to a nightclub called 'The Bunker', and now she was in the room above where several of his friends had taken turns. Could she call it rape? Probably. Was she lucky to be alive? Definitely.

She staggered out of the room, unable to find her underwear. She had saved up money for that lingerie and it had just ended up torn and discarded by hungry hands. She pulled on her skirt and clasped her blouse shut with one hand

Craig Micklewright

whilst carrying her jacket in the other. She just wanted out and going by the passed-out men lying on the floor or in other chairs, now was as good a time as any. In all honesty, she could not hate them more.

As she headed for the door, recalling a fire escape that snaked down the side of the building, a voice then called to her, interrupting her exit.

"Hey, you heading out?"

It was Carlos, that bastard … sitting in the kitchen, a near-empty bottle of rum on a table as he slumped over it. She didn't respond and twisted the knob on the door, feeling the outer cold caress her skin. It was then that she realised her wristwatch was missing, a white patch visible where she'd missed whilst applying her fake tan. There was no way she was going back into that room though. Her blouse hanging open, she quickly gave up caring if her tits were on display or not. Any self-respect she once had, was now on life support. Carlos didn't say anything further, and Lisa stepped out onto the fire escape before he could find the energy to speak again.

As it turned 2a.m Lisa walked weakly down the corridor of the apartment building, a single, torn stocking remaining on her left leg. It was like coming home from war, coming home from a war she had lost. She let herself into Tina's apartment and closed the door firmly behind her, as if to block out the still vivid images of naked and semi-naked men. As she rested her back against the door, she slowly sank to the floor and, feeling overwhelmed, burst into tears. If her

Origin

heart was to stop beating in that moment, it would be a sweet relief from the nightmare her life had become. *If only.*

*

The noises only alerted her after they had been going on for several minutes. Still lying against the door, now slouched to one side, Lisa opened her eyes. She had cried herself to sleep, exhausted from her ordeal, long dried tears crusting up her eyelids. However, a renewed energy seemed to awaken as she heard thumping and voices, mingled voices. Getting to her feet, she gathered her senses then turned to the door, twisting the handle and eased it open to allow the noise of the corridor entry.

"I tell you now, it was a horrendous racket, screaming. Late it was too, around midnight. They're two months late with their rent. I want them out. I want them out this morning!"

It was the landlord, a middle-aged woman who was always having problems with her tenants. However, this time Lisa knew she was referring to her brother, Joseph and his girlfriend, Elizabet.

Hurrying to fasten a single remaining button on her blouse, she pulled the door open to confront her landlord and defend her brother, until she discovered two Police officers in the outer corridor.

They each glanced to her as she appeared, and she was all too aware that she looked a wreck.

"Hey, what's this all about?" She asked, ignoring their staring eyes.

Craig Micklewright

Maggie, the landlord looked her up and down then stepped forward. Lisa had always got on ok with her and never had a run in, unlike Tina or the other tenants.

"Lisa! Have you seen Joseph? There was a noise coming from his apartment last night. I heard it myself and I've received complaints. You realise, I'm at my wits end with that brother of yours."

Lisa looked to the two officers, a large black guy and a smaller Korean-looking woman.

"Please go back inside, Miss. We're handling this." The large officer said then hammered his fist on the other apartment door.

Maggie stepped forward handling a large bunch of keys.

"Here, I have a key. This is ridiculous."

The officers moved aside as Maggie inserted a key in the lock then opened the door. There was a slight odour released and the large officer took a gun from his belt.

"Ok, stay back please. We'll just see what the situation is here." He remarked then walked inside, closely followed by the female officer.

Lisa lingered in her doorway as Maggie watched the open apartment door. *Had something happened?* Lisa wondered to herself and began to feel nervous. She glanced back into the apartment, not having checked the rest of the place to see if Tina was back. A raised voice was then heard coming from next door. She stepped into the corridor just as the large officer returned and began to report into his radio.

"Officer Jackson reporting in. We need a coroner. There's been an incident. Inform Sergeant Benning."

Origin

Lisa's nerves went into overdrive, and she pushed past Maggie and tried to enter the apartment. The Korean officer grabbed her firmly.

"Hey hold up there Miss. I'm afraid this is now a crime scene!"

"A crime scene? My brother lives here!" Lisa exclaimed and pulled away, rushing into the apartment.

Bursting into the bedroom, Lisa then skidded on her feet as she discovered Tina on the bed, still tied and gagged, clearly dead. Her skin was pale and her eyes were wide and motionless. In the centre of her chest, between her breasts was the dagger, imbedded in the middle of a pentagram. She went to place a hand over her mouth but wasn't quick enough, an ear shattering scream escaping that shook her to her core.

Behind, the Police officers rushed in, along with Maggie. The female officer came beside a shaking and hysterical Lisa, quick to embrace her as she turned and cried her pain onto the woman's shoulder.

Maggie, horrified walked further into the room and discovered, lying on the floor, Joseph. The male officer approached, crouched down and checked his pulse. He was alive. Maggie then alerted him.

"Look!" She exclaimed, and the officer glanced to the doorway of the altar room to see a further body concealed under a bed sheet.

"Jesus fuckin' Christ. What went on here?" He remarked.

Nobody could answer. The horror of the scene making any explanation impossible.

116

Craig Micklewright

4

arry sits at the desk within his office at his apartment in Greenwich Village. Some of the documents out of the box from the precinct, are piled before him. The file Blake obtained from Juanita is also there, and as Harry eats toast with marmalade spread liberally, he opens the file, leaving a stain on the cover. He is immediately presented with the old, faded photo of Lisa Watts. Blake was right, she'd never had the face of a killer.

He takes another bite of the toast, munching on it as crumbs coat the stubble on his chin, and thinks back to the first time he met her.

*

Origin

Harry walked down the corridor of the apartment building and stopped where the two officers were standing, now talking to a crime scene forensics guy dressed in white overalls.

"Hey, Sarge', good to see you." The forensics guy said and he and Harry shook hands.

Back then Harry's hair was dark and had only just started greying in parts along with a slight bald patch.

"Ditto, Harrison, so what we got here? I had word about a double homicide?" Harry replied looking to the black officer.

In the brief time it had taken for Harry to arrive, Lisa had changed into sweatpants and a thin jumper. She looked tired and felt even worse, the Police having not allowed her time to shower. Harry gave her the once over as the black officer filled him in.

"Two dead, both female and well Sarge, the one seems to have been killed in a kind of ritualistic fashion. The suspect, who we are only calling that for the time being, was found unconscious. Paramedics checked him over and he's unresponsive."

Harry looked into the apartment and could see two more men in overalls. Joseph's unconscious body was visible at the foot of the bed.

He then turned and looked to Lisa, "And this is?"

She looked back at him timidly.

"Suspect's sister and a close friend of one of the deceased." The officer replied.

118

Lisa appeared like a scared, traumatised little girl. Immediately Harry's heart went out to her, but any sympathy was clouded by the fact they would need to speak to her thoroughly down at the precinct.

He stepped forward offering his hand, "Sergeant Harry Benning, Miss."

Lisa looked at his hand, and then retrieved her own from where she had her arms folded and placed it in his, and they shook firmly. His hand was warm and spongy to the touch.

"Lisa... erm, Lisa Watts." She replied nervously.

"Hey, I'm sure this has been a very difficult time for you. Let's get you down to the precinct and we can have a chat. Er, do you want to freshen up first?"

Relieved, Lisa nodded then disappeared inside Tina's apartment. Harry sighed and looked back towards the other doorway.

"I want prints, hair fibres, murder weapon, the works. So get to it people! And if that guy wakes up, somebody call me straight away." He ordered then walked back the way he came.

The forensics guy and the two Police officers looked at one another, then ventured inside the apartment.

About an hour later, a refreshed-looking Lisa, her face free of make-up and her hair washed, sat at a table in an interview room at the precinct. The events of the previous night plagued her mind - how couldn't they? *That was it*, she thought, *she needed out* - Carlos wouldn't like it, but after everything, how could she go back to the streets? Tina was

Origin

dead for crying out loud. Questions buzzed through her mind like a plague of locusts.

She jolted as the door opened and Harry walked in. The noise of a bustling Police precinct flooded the room until Harry closed the door again, restoring some quiet. Lisa looked up at him, following him with her eyes until he took a seat opposite. She relaxed back in her chair.

"Miss Watts. How you doing?" He asked.

Lisa shrugged, "I have no idea. I guess I'm still processing." She replied.

"Well, the situation as it stands is, your brother has been taken to hospital. He remains unconscious. It's very strange indeed. Your friend, Miss Lawson, a name we got from the information obtained from your landlord, is dead. Do you know if your brother had any involvement in certain religious beliefs?"

Lisa looked around the room. A poster on the wall was advertising a missing persons call-line. She re-focused on Harry.

"His girlfriend, Elizabet was a wicker... do you know what that is?"

"Not exactly. You're referring to Elizabet... 'Gauthier', if I'm not mistaken ... I'm sorry to report that she was also found dead. It appears she was strangled."

Lisa bowed her head, taking in the news - she had never taken to her brother's girlfriend, but still she could never have anticipated any of this.

"She was into occult stuff, knew some folks, got hold of stuff. You know, she had a freakin' altar in their apartment. She was knee deep in that devil-shit."

"She knew folk?"

"Joseph and Elizabet used to go to parties, not long after he left hospital. She involved him in things she was a part of, but I never had anything to do with it. I had my own problems."

"Joseph Watts was in hospital?"

"Joseph's been in and out of psychiatric facilities since he was a kid. Momma ya know, used to say he was 'born wrong'."

"Your landlord happened to mention that Miss Lawson and yourself were rumoured to be prostitutes. Is that where you were last night, working?"

Lisa closed her eyes at the mention of her relatively young profession, and flashes of the assault she suffered at the hands of Carlos and his friends played out in her head like an old cine film. She ached in her loins and knew she should likely report it, but also knew if she did, she would just become another statistic.

"If I say yes, you gonna arrest me?"

Harry smiled, "I think there's more serious things going on here than a girl selling herself. Let's focus on the details. What time would you say you returned to the apartment?"

"I can't be sure. It was after 1... maybe getting on for 2a.m."

"The noises that were reported happened around midnight. So that means you wouldn't have really witnessed anything."

"No."

Origin

"Well, I'm sorry for your loss Miss Watts. I er... don't really see a reason to detain you any further. We have your details if we need to get in touch."

Lisa looked at him wide-eyed, "You're saying I'm free to go?"

"Yes. Just be careful out there. It's a dangerous world we live in."

*

Harry closes the file, reminiscing. A noise alerts him followed by muffled voices and he stands up.

Walking into the living area he sees Blake as he enters, closely followed by a young girl. Confused and suddenly self-conscious, Harry secures his dressing gown.

"Oh Harry, sorry this is 'Gemma'. Hope you don't mind me bringing her back here, it's just that, there's been a development. To put it mildly."

Gemma, her hood now down, revealing dirty-blonde hair cut into bangs, smiles at Harry, feeling a bit awkward herself.

Harry then notices how Blake is rubbing the back of his head and some dirt still covers his shirt and over coat.

"Erm, not at all er... what's with you? You been playing in the mud?" He responds.

Gemma goes about checking out the apartment, walking over to a glass cabinet that has a display of various commendations Harry has earned throughout his career. He's shown in one framed photo getting a medal. She's impressed.

Craig Micklewright

Blake walks up close to Harry, "I got jumped. It was at the cemetery, at Lisa's grave. When I awoke, I was by this lake. If Gemma here hadn't come find me, I would have no idea what happened."

"Who did it?"

"Juanita Equarez and some guy, according to my new friend here. She's been following them, and noticed they were tailing us. They have been for a day or so."

Harry glances over to Gemma who has taken out the framed photo from the cabinet and is examining it.

"Hey, put that back." He says sternly.

Jolting, Gemma looks over then quickly returns the photo to the cabinet, closing the door and offers Harry an innocent expression.

"That's not all." Blake adds, grabbing Harry's attention again, "They took it, Harry. The dagger. They stole it."

Harry returns a worried look and rubs a growing ache in his brow.

Soon they are all seated around the coffee table, Harry in his armchair, Blake and Gemma beside each other on the sofa.

"I know neither of you know me from a bag of apples, but I came here about a month back, managed to start working at the brothel. It was in the end, the best way to get close enough to Juanita Equarez to find out about her comings and goings without getting suss'. Now, I ain't proud of what I've had to do, but hear me when I say, it's got me results."

123

Origin

Blake, having wrapped some gauze around his left hand, looks enthusiastically at Harry, awaiting his response.

"By results, Miss … what do you mean?" Harry then asks.

Gemma glances to Blake who returns a subtle nod, then she leans forward, "My brother, Kai, he got in with these people. You could call them goths. I prefer the more accurate name 'weirdos'. It was about a year back. Not my kind of people … I'd rather go out in the day you see, and black has never been my colour."

"So how did you connect that to Miss Equarez?" Harry asks.

"After Kai didn't come home for weeks, my old man went sniffing around this clubhouse the Marilyn Manson freaks were known to gather at. Of course, they told my pops to clear off and he didn't get as much as a peek inside. Even dropping my brother's name hit a brick wall. So eventually we called the cops. We live on the projects of Chicago's Cabrini Green. You can probably guess how well that went - 'we'll look into it' and 'a lot of people just leave' was all they said to us."

Blake sighs, understanding.

"Yeah, there's a lot of prejudice in some precincts. Sorry you faced that." Harry says, resenting for a moment his own profession.

"After a while I decided to take a look myself, at first going over to that place when they were having one of their shindigs. I managed to talk to Kai, but we argued and well, that was the last time we saw one another. About a week later and with no more word from Kai, I broke into the place, and found some paperwork that had Juanita's name on bills and agreements and well, her address was here in the city that never sleeps. So what was a girl to do? Wait for the cops to let the case go cold? Fuck no, I decided to ship out and get answers. I told my Dad I needed time away. Didn't tell him any more than that."

Blake jumps in, "So with your brother getting caught up in all that, were you not scared with what you might be stumbling upon?"

"Not exactly. Me and Kai, we were always tight. These people turned his head though. I think he was fuckin' this one Italian girl but I'm not 100% sure on that, but with the stuff you told me, about the devil cult, I'm now more scared for Kai than myself. I just want him found."

Blake and Harry notice the emotion in the girl's hazel eyes. It was a glimpse under the hood of her otherwise tough-talking exterior. They quickly realise helping Gemma was turning out just as important as what they had been doing up until now.

Origin

5

Lisa entered through the door of Tina's apartment. It was eerily silent. Even though it was still the same place, without her friend her surroundings felt horribly empty.

She passed by Tina's bedroom and paused. She looked in through the crack of the door almost expecting to find her sleeping, like she often would be after working all night. The bed however was made, a desk with a vanity mirror on had some make-up and her i-pod. Lisa felt emotions threaten to spill over and chose to walk on, eventually entering her own room. On her unmade bed were some discarded clothes, skirts, tops, underwear - from when she had been deciding what to wear for her 'first night'. *Like it fuckin' mattered.* Any clothing, she soon learnt was just going to get torn and discarded in a hurry to violate her.

She sat down on the bed and bowed her head, placing it into her hands as she rested her elbows on her knees. *Why couldn't it have just been the way it had started for the rest of the night? Not this horror show.* She wished she had someone in her life, someone to turn to. A thought then occurred to her.

Lisa raised her head and looked to a small bedside cabinet where a lamp was situated. Sitting below the lamp, was Darren's business card, facing her direction as if calling to her. She reached forward and picked it up, turning it over and read the printed number on the reverse. Would he really be willing to help? There was only one way to find out.

Darren Maitland arrived outside his detective agency. Bringing his old, beaten-up Ford Sedan to a halt in the small car park at the front, he shut off the engine and climbed out, just as his cell began to ring.

"Darren Maitland." He answered as he readied his keys, reaching the agency's front door.

An unlit neon sign in the window read 'Blue Circle Detective Agency'.

"Darren?" came Lisa's voice.

Darren stopped short of unlocking the door, "Yes, who's this?"

"It's Lisa. From last night, I hope it's ok me calling you."

Darren was beside himself. She was calling him? As unexpected as it was, he was pleased to hear her voice.

"Ah yeah, Lisa. Hey, how are you hun?"

"I… I've been better. Er, can we meet? I kinda need someone right now and well, I didn't know who else to turn to."

Origin

Darren looked to the street as a car drove past. He then inserted the key in the door, twisting his hand to gain entry. He walked into the reception area as he continued talking – an area with a future as a brothel foyer.

"Can you come to my agency? You still got my card I presume, by knowing this number… you'll find the address is on the front."

Lisa flipped the business card over to see the agency's logo and an address below it. She smiled to herself, relieved.

"Of course. I'll be there soon. Thank you, Darren."

"No problem at all. See you shortly." His voice responded.

Darren concluded the call and lowered the phone, quickly saving the number with her name. He had felt some unexpected connection, not just because she'd made him nut harder than he had in a long time - but there was a humanity to this woman. He was glad she had chosen to turn to him, whatever the reason.

A short while later, Darren was sat in a back office as he heard the chime of his front door. The woman who had worked for him had resigned a couple of months earlier when he'd been late paying her wages for a second month. He hadn't got around to finding a replacement.

"Er… hello? Is anyone here?" A soft, angelic voice was heard and Darren placed a copy of Hustler to one side depicting a girl with short black hair, and proceeded into the reception.

Lisa appeared in stark contrast to the image he had of her, lingering in his head from their 'brief encounter'. She looked frumpy, her face free of make-up and her attire, sweatpants and a thread-bare jumper did a good job of hiding her physical assets. He tried not to think of her like that, attempting to push the sex to the back of his mind. She seemed so beyond herself and lost.

"Lisa." He remarked, walking around the reception desk to greet her.

He brought his hands up to her shoulders and she looked to him, doe-eyed and fragile. Something had clearly gone on since he saw her last.

"What is it? Something wrong? I must admit, I never expected to get a call from you, let alone see you again."

"There's nobody else I could go to. The Police…" She replied.

"Police?"

"Yeah, my friend, Tina was er… she was found dead this morning. They think. Shit, this is hard…"

"Take your time." Darren added with compassion, letting go of her and rested against the front of the desk looking her over - she was clearly distraught.

"They think my brother, Joseph is responsible. I don't know what to think. He's had his problems but murder? I don't think he'd do anything like that."

Darren nodded, "So, did the Police interview you?"

"Yeah, some old guy, says his name was Benning."

Origin

"Ah right, I know Harry Benning. Old friend of mine. I could make some enquiries, see what they have on your brother, if you'd like?"

Lisa looked to him with a renewed hope to her eyes.

"Do you want a coffee? Have you had breakfast?"

Lisa looked down at her hands as she played with the hem of her jumper where some cotton hung, "Not yet. Yeah, I could do with some caffeine."

"I know a place. Here let's get you fed and then we'll figure a plan." Darren said getting up, and walked over to his jacket, retrieving it from a hook on the wall.

Soon they were sat either side of a table in a local diner. A clearly hungrier than she realised Lisa tucked into some pancakes with maple syrup and Darren watched her with amusement.

"When's the last time you ate pancakes?"

Lisa looked up, her mouth full and struggled to respond, "It's been a while." She muffled, then swallowed what was in her mouth before taking a gulp of coffee.

"So, tell me something, why haven't you got anyone else to turn to? Surely, I'm just another client to you…"

Lisa sighed, "Hardly. I have my Ma but, I haven't spoken to her in over a year. She's over on Staten Island. There's … there's kind of a bad history…." - briefly a memory flashed in her head of when she was younger, standing before a mirror fastening buttons on a green and white uniform as a large man observed her from behind, "Let's just say turning to my Ma, it would be a last resort. I'm not quite there yet."

Craig Micklewright

"Well, like I said I'm willing to help but I'm going to need some background. Did Joseph know your friend?"

"Yeah, they were next door neighbours in the same apartment building. I've been staying there with Tina for about two months now, but at the moment, the place is kind of a crime scene."

"Oh right. I uh, have a spare room if that would be better?"

Lisa went to eat some more pancakes when she paused, staring at Darren. *Wow*, she thought. *Who was this guy?*

"Oh, thanks but, I can't put you out. And anyway, isn't that a wedding ring?" She responded, then shoved the fork in her mouth.

Darren instinctively covered his hand with his other hand. Sometimes he would forget he was still wearing it.

"Oh, yeah but… my wife she, she left me a while back. I guess I've never really liked the idea of taking it off."

"Oh, I'm sorry. I didn't mean to pry."

"It's fine. So like I was saying, I got this big ol' house and a spare room. You're welcome to stay. If my cop days are anything to go by, your brother's apartment will be a hive of activity for the next week or so and not ideal for you to be staying next door. It would make me happy knowing you're safe and have somewhere to lay your head."

"You were a cop?"

"Once upon a time, yeah. But I quit about six months back, decided to go it alone."

"Ok then. I'll need to swing by Tina's beforehand, gotta get my things."

"I'll drive you over after this, then."

Origin

Lisa nodded as she took another mouthful of pancake.

*

Blake observes Gemma as she sits eating a grilled-cheese sandwich at a table in the kitchen of Harry's apartment. He smirks as she stuffs a crust in her mouth. She looks up on hearing and swallows, barely chewing.

"What?" She asks with a frown.

Blake, a bandage still wrapped around his hand, takes a sip of orange juice, before placing the glass on the table.

"Oh nothing. You just reminded me of someone. A woman I used to know. She was a few years older than you but had the same, erm, etiquette when eating."

"That one you were visiting the grave of?" Gemma asks.

Blake looks disturbed, "You're a very smart young woman. Yeah, she's the reason I'm back here after being gone for years."

"Oh, what happened to her?"

"She was killed, and I'm getting the impression Juanita knows more than she's letting on with what went down back then, the satanic stuff and well, that dagger was a factor, and now it's in her hands."

"Like I told you and grandpa before, Juanita and her cronies, some of the guys who work for her are planning something."

"As much as I hate to say this, Gemma, you're gonna have to act like nothing's changed. Show up for work and find out a meeting place or whatever. They must have wanted that dagger really bad to almost kill me for it."

Gemma smiles and takes a sip of coke, "You can count on me, man." She replies, "I tell you now, that witch is balls-deep in whatever happened to my brother, so consider me your right hand, girl-Friday."

Blake can't help but admire her sass, even if he feels nervous involving a girl so young, no matter her street smarts. He goes to drink his orange juice again and notices blood seep from the wound on his hand.

"Hey, you're bleeding." Gemma remarks.

Blake checks his hand, applying a napkin, "I know. I got it at the cemetery. It was only a nick, but it keeps opening back up."

"You should get it looked at."

"Maybe."

Wiping the blood away, he grabs the juice again and gulps down the remainder.

Origin

6

Darren approached the corridor at the apartment building and could hear the sound of Police radios. He looked down it to see a uniformed officer stationed outside a door where Police tape closed off the entrance. He glanced back to Lisa as she lingered nervously around the corner.

"Come on, what's up? I know, it's difficult but we'll be in and out then we can go back to mine." He said and walked forward as Lisa followed behind.

As he reached the officer, they greeted each other with recognition.

"Maitland, what you doing here?" The officer asked, a Chinese looking man.

He then noticed Lisa.

"Oh, you two acquainted?" The officer added.

Craig Micklewright

Darren smiled, "In a manner of speaking. We're here to pick up some of the lady's things. So, what's the story here?"

"Double homicide. I'm 'fraid nobody's allowed in. But understand if I can't go into details, man. It's not like you're one of us anymore. So, anyway, did you ever hear off Eleanor?"

Darren looked troubled at the mention of his wife's name, "Nothing." He replied bluntly.

"Fuckin' weird that shit was. Her just uppin' and clearing out like she did. She not even letting her Mom know?"

Lisa met up with them and lingered outside Tina's apartment.

"Well erm, we won't be long. Hey, give my best to Harry, will you?" Darren responded and turned away as Lisa unlocked the door, venturing inside.

"Will do. Hey, drop by sometime I'm sure the Sarge' would like to catch up." The officer shouted in reply, as Darren followed Lisa into the apartment.

Inside, Lisa hurried to her bedroom and pulled out an old, tattered hold-all from beneath her bed. Darren lingered in the doorway and observed. He didn't really know this woman, and had wondered what he was getting into by helping her. But something about her made him want to help, if for no other reason than to give his life some much needed purpose.

"Want me to do anything?"

Lisa placed the hold-all on the bed, starting to stuff clothes, make up, shoes etc into it. As Darren watched, he got deja-vu of his wife Eleanor, doing the same, although she had packed a suitcase rather than a bag.

Origin

"No, it's fine. This won't take long." Lisa replied, and turned, brushing past him and proceeded into Tina's room.

She grabbed a watch, just a cheap plastic Swatch and not as fancy as the one she'd lost, but it would have to do. She then noticed something glinting on a shelf as she put it on - a folded switchblade. Picking it up, she opened it and the blade sprung out sporting a serrated edge. Darren then appeared, surprised to see her with a knife.

"Woh, that yours?"

"Tina's but, considering recent events, a girl can never be too careful."

She twirled it around in her hand before folding it shut. Darren was a little unnerved but decided not to say anything further.

Tossing the hold-all into the boot of his Sedan, Darren closed the hatch, then walked around to the driver's side and joined Lisa in the front.

"Next stop... shay-Maitland." He announced with a grin, and as he went to adjust the gear stick, Lisa placed her hand over his.

Darren looked at her and she smiled attractively.

"You didn't have to do any of this, Darren but... thank you." She said before leaning forward to kiss him on the lips, a kiss that progressed and their tongues duelled, tasting each other's saliva.

When they parted, both their faces were flushed.

"It's er... my pleasure." He stammered as she moved her hand to his thigh, caressing it.

He felt himself responding, his erection straining against the confines of his trousers. Looking at her for a few seconds longer, he chose to start the car's engine rather than give into his base instincts. Lisa, realising that any proper 'thank you' could wait, sat back and secured her seat belt.

Eventually the front door of Darren's house located in Brooklyn opened, the outer daylight flooding a hallway leading to a tall white staircase. There was a pile of mail on a welcome mat, but Darren chose to ignore it as he approached the stairs - then paused. Lisa followed and came to his side, appreciating the decor; pastel-coloured walls, framed paintings of scenery, an oval mirror next to a coat stand.

"Darren?" She asked as she picked up on his hesitation.

"I only really stay here occasionally. I've mostly been sleeping at the agency."

"Really?"

As if snapping back to reality, he turned and smiled, holding her weighty hold-all in one hand.

"Anyway, let me show you to your room." He said and began to ascend.

Lisa nodded enthusiastically and followed.

A door opened to reveal a fold up bed, propped against a wall below a window. An ancient looking closet took up the majority of another wall and there was a lamp located on a small table.

Lisa observed the room - *this is perfect*, she thought. Darren then dropped her bag, making her jolt and she looked back at him.

Origin

"I'll get you some linen. Should be some downstairs." He said and walked away, leaving Lisa to wander into the room and run her finger over a radiator, discovering almost an inch of dust.

*

Lisa found herself unable to sleep. The noise had kept her awake and as she lay in bed, her head on a lumpy pillow - a repetitive banging prevented any hope of drifting off. Opening her eyes, she noticed a closet door banging in a breeze. Exhaling her frustration, she sat up and pulled the covers away. Wearing just a T-shirt she got up, padded across cold wood flooring, reached to the closet door and went to close it - until she noticed something peeking out. The sleeve of an outfit, green in colour. Confused, she opened the door to reveal her majorette uniform from when she was thirteen. *How? What on earth?*

She glanced back to the window beside her bed. The drapes moved slightly. She turned back and took the uniform from inside and held it up… it was definitely her uniform, but that was impossible!

"Try it on." A gentle voice then said.

She looked back, holding the uniform by its hanger and discovered a large figure standing at the foot of the fold-out bed. She strained her eyes to make it out, until it stepped into a beam of light coming in from between the drapes. It was none other than her Father. He was an oafish man, wearing glasses and had black hair in a comb-over. He looked at her with that look which had appeared as she grew. Once she had

Craig Micklewright

started to develop, his interest began. He had always been affectionate but… this was something else.

"Daddy?" She remarked in disbelief as he approached and reached up and pulled at her t-shirt.

"You can look prettier, Lisa. Take this old thing off."

Lisa screwed her face up with reluctance, "No, I'm embarrassed." She replied, but he continued to pull at the t-shirt.

"Alright, I'll look away. Get changed now dear…"

He turned away and she reluctantly removed her t-shirt, then, just in her knickers, began to put on the uniform, which by all reasoning should be far too small, but as it turned out, fitted perfectly. Pulling on matching knee-length socks and fastening the pleated skirt around her waist, she turned to her father for inspection. He turned to look at her, eyes leering, exploring. He reached up and ran his dirty fingers over polished metal buttons, and gently brushed the swell of her breasts.

"You're maturing right before my eyes. You're becoming a woman." He said, running his hand down her body and delved under her skirt. Lisa gasped as he cupped her between her legs. His hand was firm, pressing and his fingers rubbed. Without wanting it, her body reacted. He was making her wet.

"Face the closet now, sweetie."

"Daddy, I don't…"

"Closet, now!" He demanded with a firmer tone.

Feeling tears imminent in her eyes she turned on her heels and he pressed her against the closet door. She gasped as he lifted her skirt and impatiently yanked down her knickers. She waited, hearing him fumble with his own clothing, the clink

Origin

of a belt buckle, and then he was grunting and panting. He didn't put it in, not this time... but he was doing something else. He was moving his hand between their bodies in a feverish action, then after only a short while, she felt something wet hit her bare behind. He exhaled against her neck, his breath making the light hairs dance, his weight overbearing as he calmed himself ... and after another minute, he moved away.

With tears rolling down her cheeks she eventually reached down to pull her knickers up from where they had bunched around her knees, and turned to see that her father was gone.

She walked, trembling beside the bed then came to a full-length mirror. Stepping before it, she was presented by her reflection, albeit when she was thirteen years old, an innocent, troubled face looking back at her.

"You've always seen yourself as the victim..." a deep voice then said, its tone rumbling through the room like the strum of a bass guitar.

"You blamed yourself for your father's advances and have continued throughout your life to only see your worth as the object of male desire. This led to numerous high school fumblings and countless one-night stands, before finally selling yourself to any man willing to offer you money."

Her reflection gradually transformed, and she was standing before herself wearing the t-shirt again and an adult.

"Who are you?" She said out loud.

"A traveller between realms. A student in the furthest reaches of experience."

A nervous Lisa then stepped to one side, revealing to her continued unease, a cloaked figure, a hood concealing its face. A sudden drop in temperature made her shiver.

"W-What do you want?"

"I'm here to offer you an out. A way to escape your self-loathing, your misery and to exact retribution."

"Retribution?"

"The men, who assaulted you... at the club. It has scarred your mind, not just your body. Ask yourself... do they really deserve to go on living for what they did?"

Lisa looked to the figure, a cold fear dancing in her belly.

"I-I couldn't ... I could never."

A hand grasped her shoulder, its fingernails like claws, "It'll be alright my child, I will give you the strength."

Lisa closed her eyes tightly, urging the figure away. Suddenly she was back in bed, sweating and shaking. She looked again to the closet, the door standing open. Her uniform however, was gone. Instantly, she buried herself beneath the covers and wept.

Origin

7

The following morning, Darren walked out of his room wearing boxers and a t-shirt. Bleary-eyed and yawning, he proceeded into the bathroom. Inside he began to unbutton his shirt, and before long, stepped under the spray, naked and let out a groan as the soothing warmth engulfed him.

As he stood there, hands pressed to the tiles, under the shower head … in the background a figure moved… just a shadow… but someone for sure. Darren ignorantly continued to wallow in the spray, unaware as the shower screen slid open, until arms then slowly wrapped around him. Gasping at their touch, he noticed a reflection of someone on the water-drenched tiles, female, a woman, and she moved behind him, her body naked and rubbing against his. Looking down, his vision blurred by the spray of water he saw a hand wrap fingers around his penis, massaging it until it grew and stiffened.

Lisa came up close to his ear and started kissing and nibbling. Darren was surprised but appreciative, and as she jerked his erection, he let out a groan. Damn, her hand knew what it was doing. He turned around, his eyes exploring her face as beads of water ran down it. *She was so beautiful*, he thought. Their mouths came together in a lazy, lingering kiss, any words were unnecessary.

He pushed her against the cubical door. She let out a grunt, opening her eyes and returned a cheeky grin as he lift her leg with his hand under her knee and she guided him towards her opening, until he slid effortlessly inside her. Letting out a sigh as he filled her, his hips began grinding and they kissed again, this time not simply fucking, but actually making love. As the water drenched their bodies and they slid against one other, writhing in sync, they almost felt like the same person; their bodies moulding together in erotic perfection.

As passion intensified, Darren's thrusts became harder and Lisa couldn't help but yelp and moan, his rigid phallus rubbing and stretching her - *it felt incredible*. The cubical began to shake and creek, until Lisa was being pounded with a violence that they both craved, almost without realising. They needed this. They needed each other, to push bad thoughts and bad memories, troubled lives to the back of their minds, forced away in place of sexual fulfillment. Reaching the crescendo of their passion, they climaxed simultaneously, gasping into each other's mouths as the tingling rush of orgasm trembled through their bodies.

Origin

Afterwards, Lisa stood alone in the bathroom. Steam lingered in the air all around as she rubbed her hair with a towel, naked before a wash basin, the mirror coated in condensation making her reflection barely definable. Despite the pain and murkiness of recent events, at least one thing was feeling right. Something was starting between herself and Darren, something positive. She hoped it remained that way.

Discarding the towel and stepping closer to the wash basin, she reached her hand to the mirror to wipe the condensation away, then jolted to find Joseph standing behind her. She turned around suddenly. He was in the bathroom with her. She fell against the wash basin, unable to believe her eyes and instinctively covered her breasts with her hands.

"What are you doing here?" She asked.

"I'm not here, not really. I'm in a coma, sis…" Joseph replied, himself shirtless, his tribal tattoo striking on his right arm.

"I don't understand."

"There is work to be done. You have to sacrifice their lives, to free me, to save me, and to save yourself. You're our only hope."

"How could you… to Tina?"

Joseph looked troubled by her question, "I never wanted any of that, you need to believe me. It was Elizabet…"

"She made you do it?"

"Not exactly. I-I killed Elizabet. But it was an accident! The demon, he…"

"You've seen him too?"

Joseph looked at her, shocked, "Yes, Lisa. I've seen him. He requires five sacrifices. Tina was the first. Four more souls and then, you and I will both be set free."

Lisa turned away, hurrying to dress, grabbing her knickers from a stool and stepped into them, pulling them up to her waist, then grabbed her t-shirt, pulling that on over her head.

"Listen to me, Lisa. You have to do this or the suffering, that we will both endure, will be never ending."

"It's already never ending for me." She mumbled back, turning to face her brother.

"What do you mean?"

Briefly, she felt their father's breath on the back of her neck again. She shuddered.

"Nothing. It doesn't matter."

Joseph reached out and took her hand in his, squeezing.

"Kill four more and we will be free. Please Lisa, don't leave me to suffer."

She closed her eyes then felt him let go of her. After a moment she opened her eyes to discover she was once again alone. A knock came to the door, and she looked to it as Darren poked his head in.

"Hey, I'm heading off to the agency. I think I'll contact Sergeant Benning and see if he'll give up some info, for old times' sake… you erm, you ok?"

Lisa just stared at him, like she was looking through him. Her eyes then focused on his face, "Yeah. I'm fine."

"Wanna come along?" Darren asked.

She shook her head, "No, I think I'll just relax here or take a walk out. It's my head, think I just need some time to myself, after everything."

Origin

Darren, having put on a shirt and trousers, stepped inside the bathroom and leaned close, kissing her on her cheek.

"Alright. I'll be back later. You have my number if you need me." He said, running his hand affectionately down her arm, then walked back out.

Lisa couldn't shake the thoughts in her head. Something was churning inside her, deep in her belly. If she was going to do this, if she could even contemplate it, Darren could never find out. Those men did deserve to die. They did deserve to be killed. She would never again be treated like she was worthless. She would teach them her worth. Those fuckers had it coming.

*

Gemma sits on the bed at the brothel. Wearing a long gown, she entwines her legs as feet peek out in fishnets. A little too much make-up splatters her face with dark eyeliner that makes her appear gothic. She feels like she always does before a client is due to join her... willing herself to switch off emotionally and just let him do his thing, whoever he turns out to be.

A knock comes to the door. The bed she sits on is the centre piece of a small room. Blood-red lamp light casts a glow over silk-effect sheets, and she pushes a condom packet out of sight under a pillow as she looks over.

"Come in baby." She says, a pulse of nerves rearing its head as the door opens.

Craig Micklewright

A small, ageing man walks in wearing a suit and smiles as he approaches the bed. Gemma stands up and goes to greet him until he touches the side of her face and grins.

"Oh, you're a cute thing. You have pretty eyes." He comments.

Gemma blushes slightly, turning to the bed and bends over to straighten the sheets.

"Why don't you get undressed honey, and we'll make ourselves comfortable."

He then comes behind her, grabbing her hips and draws her gown up to expose her ass in a g-string. She flinches, looking back to him, "Now now Mister, no need to rush…"

"Less of the Mister…" He says, "Call me Uncle Henry."

Gemma frowns.

Minutes after, one of the other girls passes by the room just as she hears someone cry out. Suddenly the door bursts open and the man stumbles out, his trousers around his ankles and he's nursing a bloody nose. He hurries to pull his trousers up and rushes past the girl, complaining loudly. The girl then peers in to see Gemma standing by the bed.

"What?" Gemma remarks, "He wanted me to play act at being his niece!"

The girl just stares at her, shocked.

Soon after Gemma stands in an office before a large desk. Behind is Juanita looking at her sternly.

"This is the second time you've assaulted a client, Gemma. You do realise, we are not here to pass judgement on whatever warped perversions they have swimming around in

Origin

their heads. We provide a service and more often than not that means catering to the desires these men can't act out in their day to day lives. Who is to say, you haven't just enabled that freak to actually try molesting his niece, instead of getting it out of his system by fucking you?"

Gemma wrinkles her face up, "When you put it like that, I guess you have a point. I just didn't like how he was looking at me. It felt like I was in grade school again fending off the advances of a far too hands-on gym teacher."

Juanita sighs, leaning forward and opens a file, leafing through the pages until she comes to Gemma's profile.

"You came to us last month, without a cent to your name and in need of the kind of work that doesn't ask questions." She says, eyes scanning what's typed below a small passport-like photo, "Overall, clients like you. So I'm willing to give you one last chance but, if I hear of anything like this again, I'm sorry Gemma, but I have the house's reputation to consider, and clients can't be coming here thinking they're going to leave with a black eye."

"Don't worry Juanita. I promise you it won't happen again."

A knock comes to the door and Gemma looks back as it opens and Drago peers in. He was a man who had intimidated Gemma from day one and today was no different.

"Juanita, got something to discuss, it's important."

"Ok, back to work Gemma." Juanita orders and Gemma hurries away, briefly making eye contact with the large, towering Spaniard as she leaves.

Outside as the door closes, Gemma lingers then hears them talking and leans close to eves-drop, pressing her ear to the wood. As she listens, gradually her eyes widen in astonishment. Unbeknownst to her, a small security camera peers down from the ceiling, disguised as a lighting fixture.

"The eclipse is around eight thirty tonight, Juanita. Are you sure we have everything ready? If tonight doesn't go to plan, we'll have no use for him. I tell you now, we didn't bring his ass over from Chicago just to dump him in a landfill."

Gemma steps away from the door as she hears movement then hurries down the corridor. Hiding in the doorway of another room, she watches as Drago exits with Juanita.

"Ok I'll head back to my place, then go over there in the next hour or so, keep an eye on him. It'd be wise if you came along. We need to get everything ready. We miss this and that'll be it, our opportunity will be gone." He says and walks away.

Juanita watches him go then ventures back into her office just as Gemma steps out from the doorway, her brain working overtime.

Origin

8

arry Benning was handed a leather-bound book as he stood in the bedroom of Joseph and Elizabet's apartment.

"What's this?" He asked as a young black Police officer stood beside him.

The bed, now absent of Tina's body was still draped with blood-stained sheets.

"That comatose son-of-a-bitch was holding onto it for dear life. Interesting thing is, wait till you open it up."

Harry opened the book to reveal that, although the pages appeared old and faded, they were all blank.

"What am I looking at here?"

"Damned if I know. There's more in the other room. Gotta say, Sarge' this case has freaked me out."

Harry closed the book, running a finger over the embossed image on the cover resembling a goat's head with

Craig Micklewright

huge horns. He tossed it onto the bed and followed the officer as he walked through the bedroom and entered the adjoining room where Elizabet's altar sat.

"Jesus Christ." Harry remarked as he set eyes on the candles and unnerving imagery.

"What were these two into? This looks like something out of the dark ages."

"You said before that the sister, Lisa Watts told you the girl who lived here referred to herself as a 'wicker' and was known to dabble in satanism. If you ask me, this world is better off having one less of those twisted freaks walking around."

Harry looked from the altar to the officer then walked back out.

As he ventured into the apartment's hallway, passing by a kitchen on-route to the front door, he looked up as someone knocked on the doorframe. He instantly recognised Darren standing beyond the Police tape in the outer corridor.

"Maitland, what are you doing here?"

"Would you believe I was just passing?" Darren replied.

"Not entirely." Harry said then ducked under the tape to stand with Darren in the corridor.

"Ok you got me. I'm kinda stumbling on this whole thing. I've become acquainted with the sister of the guy who lives here."

"Oh really?"

"Yeah. So, I thought I'd come see how the investigation's going, thought you might let me in on it, you know, us being old friends an' all."

151

Origin

"Friends now huh? You didn't turn to me when your wife left you, and then you gave your badge in to the Superintendent without saying a word."

Darren walked a few steps down the corridor, "Yeah, I'm sorry about that, I was going through some stuff."

"Well, I can't involve you in this, Darren. It'd be more than my job's worth and we're still kinda scratching our heads over it anyway."

Darren looked back to Harry, his former mentor and someone he still admired, "That makes sense but, whether I like it or not, I am involved now and would like to help in any way I can. Lisa is really cut up about it all. This was her best friend and her brother."

Harry sighed, approaching, "Maybe I can see if there is anything you can do, strictly off the books. You used to be a good cop, after all."

Darren smiled with a heavy heart, "Back in the day, maybe. Now though? I'm just trying to keep from putting a gun in my mouth."

Harry looked concerned, "I hope that's a joke."

Darren smirked and walked on, "Just call me. My number's never changed." He answered then turned the corner, leaving Harry's line of sight.

*

A melody is heard playing in Harry's apartment and Blake exits a bathroom. Securing a fresh bandage around his hand, he is quick to answer his cell where he'd left it on the coffee table. From the kitchen, Harry emerges eating from a bowl of porridge.

"Is that…"

"It's Gemma." Blake replies then switches the call to speaker.

"We're both here kid, myself and Harry."

"Hey guys. I can't stay on long. I got some news. You're gonna want to get on this straight away I think."

Blake checks his watch, noticing that it was just gone 6p.m. Looking at his hand he turns it to reveal a red stain on the bandage where it covers his palm. He lets out a sigh of frustration.

"Ok, what you got for me?" He then asks.

Outside the brothel, Gemma stands catching the breeze, her hood up.

"I managed to hear some stuff." She reports, lowering her voice, "This big fuckin' dude called 'Drago', he's going some place later. They're holding someone, a hostage I think, and it's all to do with the eclipse that's happening tonight. They said they brought him over from Chicago. That's where I'm from, and where Kai went missing. Listen to me when I say, this ain't no fuckin' coincidence, I can feel it in ma' shit!"

Blake looked to Harry, "The eclipse, huh?" - Harry looks intrigued, "Er… do you have an address for this Drago guy?"

"Lives out in Queens." Gemma continues, "I got introduced to the guy first night I got the job. Let's just say that donkey-dick motherfucker can't get hard unless you piss

Origin

on him first. You ever tried squatting over someone's face and meant to be in the mood to open the flood gates? Fuckin' wouldn't happen, would it? Then I was handed a jug of water…."

Blake can't help but smirk, "Ok, Gemma, I get the picture. Tell me where I can find him, and we'll see if we can do an old school stake out."

"My fuckin' thoughts exactly, man." Gemma replies with a smile.

Just then, the side door of the brothel opens and one of the girls peers out.

"Hey Gem' we got this client coming in, willing to pay big bucks for two girls, you up for a bit of overtime?"

"I'll text you an address. I gotta go now." She concludes into the phone, then ends the call as she looks to the girl.

"Ok but this time, no biting." She responds.

*

Lisa walked down the street towards an illuminated nightclub, a large neon sign read 'The Bunker'. Slowing her walk, high heels scraping on the sidewalk, she stepped under the glow of a streetlamp just as a door opened and a man stumbled out, his arm around a young-looking Hispanic girl. Lisa was startled to recognise him as one of *those men* from the other night… this one having been particularly rough with her.

"You gotta be kiddin' me." She remarked under her breath, beginning to approach, painting her best fake smile on her face as the man noticed her.

"Hey, don't I know you, sweetheart?" He said.

He was Mexican, well-built with a goatee. Lisa reached him, strong perfume drifting under his nose. He relinquished his hold on the girl who looked at Lisa with disdain.

"Who's this?" She asked.

The man kept his eyes focused as he answered the girl, "Someone that's telling me, we're not going back to mine after all."

He shoved the girl away as he reached out to Lisa. She offered her hand, and he took it gently.

"Marco, what's got into you?"

Marco leered at Lisa thirstily, "Fuck off Imelda." He responded, and a clearly disgruntled Imelda stormed off back to the club.

Soon they were walking to a black SUV, Marco gentlemanly opening the passenger door and helping her inside. As she climbed in, he slapped the swell of her ass in her leather mini skirt. He then joined her in the front cabin and grabbed her thigh, giving it a firm squeeze.

"If it's any consolation, babe I never intended the party the other night to go like it did. I was drunk but not as drunk as some of the others. Carlo was out of order; I told him that much. You were treated like trash. I suspect you're worth more than that."

The words would have been comforting if this man hadn't been equally as guilty. She still found herself wincing in pain

Origin

every time she visited the toilet. He was a fuckin' animal just like the rest. An animal that needed putting down.

"Oh, forget about it. It's in the past. Anyway, you were my favourite." She said with fake sincerity.

"Is that so?" Marco responded, turning to her and ran his hand up her leg, over her ribs and cupped her breast.

"Let's go back to yours." She added, then leaned towards him and they kissed.

The taste of his breath mixed with a lack of hygiene was nearly enough to make her vomit.

Darren returned to his house, calling out for Lisa as he entered. He walked into the living room to see the TV on playing an episode of Breaking Bad. Venturing back into the hallway he sprinted up the staircase then paused where it turned a corner at the top. Something made him stop. He looked back to see Eleanor with a suitcase making her way down. He watched her descend just as a vision of himself followed and grabbed her arm. Eleanor turned to look at him just as the memory faded. Steadying himself with a hand to the bannister, Darren, slightly unnerved took a deep breath and proceeded onto the upstairs hallway.

"Lisa, you in?" He called then stopped at the door to the spare room, opposite the bathroom.

Pushing the door inwards, he ventured inside as it brushed the carpet to discover a neatly made bed, along with various items of clothing draped upon it. Some make up sat on a cabinet next to a lamp. He looked around but it was obvious Lisa wasn't home.

Craig Micklewright

Her hand frantically jerked his hard penis as her tongue flickered on the bulbous tip, and he gritted his teeth with intense pleasure. Without warning, semen erupted to splash her lips and chin. Lisa gasped, spitting out any that got in her mouth, and slowed her movements, his once mighty erection wilting like a deflating balloon animal. With a groan Marco lay back on the bed, closing his eyes with satisfaction.

"Damn, I came like a comet!" He exclaimed breathlessly.

Sitting up, she applied some tissue to wipe away the excess semen as it dripped from her chin.

She looked at him as he relaxed, naked, barrel chested, spent. Wearing only her black stockings, her own body seeming to glow in the subdued lamplight, she moved to sit astride him and took a lipstick from her coat where it lay, crumpled next to Marco's legs. She then reached down and began to draw on his wide chest.

Marco sniggered, "Hey, what's that you're doing?"

"Oh, just marking my territory." Lisa answered.

Marco smiled, enjoying the game then after a moment, opened his eyes - immediately, he was presented with his reflection in a large mirror fixed to the ceiling. A pentagram had been drawn on his chest in red lipstick.

"Hang on, what the fuck?" He exclaimed and went to sit up until Lisa shoved him back down, suddenly revealing the switchblade.

"Fuck me!" He gasped, quick to reach out and snatch her wrist in his hand as she went to drive the blade down.

With his other hand he slugged her across the face. Lisa toppled from the bed, and Marco got up, rushing to where

Origin

his clothes were piled on a chair next to where an electric guitar stood upright on a stand. He reached into a jacket and pulled out a revolver.

All of a sudden Lisa leaped off the bed onto him, screaming like a banshee and sank the knife into his shoulder. Crying out, Marco turned and tossed her effortlessly against the wall. She hit a large painting, knocking it from the wall as she fell to the floor with a grunt. Staggering, Marco reached to the blade in his shoulder and pulled it out, looking at it as it dripped blood before tossing it aside. He then aimed the gun to where Lisa lay.

"What the hell?!? You try and kill me? You fuckin' crazy bitch!"

He landed a kick to her stomach, and she cried out in agony.

"We should have ended you after we all used you, like the worthless whore that you are! You ain't good for nothing but to be fucked and discarded. You made a big fuckin' mistake thinking you could take revenge." He said as he pulled back the hammer on the revolver, finger resting, itching on the trigger.

A gentle chuckle was heard, and he looked with confusion. As he watched, Lisa's head turned and snapped to face the wrong way, and slowly she stood up, her arms pulling inwards, the bones cracking as they bent backwards. Horrified, Marco squeezed the trigger just as his gun melted inexplicably in his hand, and he let go as it burnt his skin.

Backing off to the bed, he watched in disbelief as Lisa stood before him, her legs turning in on themselves with a horrible crunch noise. Her breasts formed across her back as her spine and shoulder blades sank inward, replaced by the bulge of her ribs and the swell of her belly. Finally, her ass sank into her flesh to form a neatly groomed groin. Lisa was then suddenly facing Marco, having not turned around at all.

Marco looked up her body and focused on her face just as her pupils glowed bright yellow.

"What the hell are you?!?!" He gasped.

Lisa didn't reply as she raised a hand to catch her switchblade as it flew to her like metal drawn to a magnet. With a gleeful grin, she then thrust the blade into his chest, right in the centre of the pentagram.

9

Lisa entered through the front door of Darren's house. She stood near a coat stand and noticed her reflection in the mirror on the wall. Examining her face, there was a slight swelling to her cheek where Marco had hit her. Proceeding to her chin, she ran fingertips over her skin. It was gone … that creature. Whatever was now part of her, it was asleep, dormant … for the time being.

She eased off her leather jacket, the front of her thin blouse a little unbuttoned, cleavage exposed. She hung her jacket up and proceeded towards the staircase.

Suddenly Darren appeared in the doorway of the living room, his face the picture of concern.

"Where have you been?" He asked, a slightly accusing tone to his words.

"Out."

Craig Micklewright

Darren glanced to an antique-looking clock, "It's almost midnight. You're telling me you were 'working'? Not after what happened…"

Lisa went to ascend the stairs, not in the right mind to get into anything, "I'm tired Darren. Can I just go to bed?"

He came to the wooden post at the bottom of the stairs as she paused one step up, "I saw Harry Benning today. He's agreed to let me lend a hand. Good news, huh?"

Lisa thought it best not to look at him, "Yes that is good. I gotta get some sleep now." She replied and proceeded upstairs.

Darren watched her go. *Damn she's looking good*, he thought as he turned away. He hoped he'd be able to help her in some way, at the very least give her some closure. Walking back into the living room, a bed was made up on the couch, showing he wasn't quite up to returning to the marital bed, if he ever would be. Apart from providing Lisa with a roof over her head away from the noise of the investigation, he still wasn't comfortable being back in the house, not without Eleanor.

He sat down on the makeshift bed and looked to see his wife dancing in her nightie, music gradually filling the room. The memory was from shortly after they moved in… days after their wedding. Happier times. Darren closed his eyes tightly, relaxing back and allowed himself to doze, willing the images and thoughts to the dark recesses of his mind.

Lisa stepped into her bedroom and slipped out of her high heels. The soft carpet soothed the souls of her feet, and she

Origin

sat down on the fold out bed. Crossing one leg over the other, she proceeded to roll a stocking down to her ankle before peeling it off. She then did the same with the other before rolling the nylon into balls and tossing them to the floor. She was aching from her exhaustion - but the night wasn't done with her yet. A presence washed over her as she sat, contemplating her actions. Did she feel guilty? Not exactly. Did she feel bad she had taken a life? Shocked she was even capable, more like.

"You have performed admirably." The demon's voice then rumbled through the room.

Lisa didn't look up, focusing on her feet as they sat flat on the carpet. A shard of moonlight beamed in, the single illumination in the small room. She dare not look up. She didn't want to see its face.

"I did as was asked of me." She replied quietly.

"Three more and then you can claim your freedom." The demon continued.

Lisa nodded, "If that is how it must be. Joseph has suffered enough all his life."

"That is how it must be, child."

Lisa sighed as a cold breeze announced the demon's departure and she shivered before slowly unbuttoning her blouse. Discarding it to a chair, leaving her bra on, bruises were evident on her back and abdomen. She then stood up and removed her skirt before climbing into bed.

"Just let me sleep." She asked out loud then turned to face the wall, pulling the covers over her head.

Craig Micklewright

*

Darren was awoken by his phone ringing. He had fallen asleep fully dressed on the couch and he slowly sat up and fumbled around the bedclothes until he spotted his cell lying on the floor beside his feet. He reached down and answered it.

"Maitland."

"Darren? It's Harry. You said to call you if I had anything. Well, it looks like we got another victim."

Darren rubbed his eyes then stood up, "What do you mean? Lisa gave me the impression you guys were pointing the finger at her brother."

"Considering that guy's still in his coma and under Police surveillance, we might be looking at another killer."

Darren stumbled out into the hallway, proceeding into the kitchen and switched on a coffee machine. He ran the faucet on the sink, swilling out a mug as he replied.

"Where you at?"

"Hell's Kitchen."

After a moment, in the spare room Lisa jolted as a knock came to her door. She rolled over and looked across the room as the door clicked open. She pushed the covers away slightly as Darren peered in.

"Hey. You ok, hun?" He asked.

Waking to see his face was comforting. She gradually sat up as an early morning sun bathed her, and stretched her arms

Origin

above her head, breasts bulging out of her bra. Darren came to her bedside, peering down at her.

"I have to go out. Just got a call from Harry, you know... Sergeant Benning. Looks like there's been another murder. Says it looks like the same killer."

Lisa wrinkled her brow as she dropped her arms - briefly she pictured Marco's body, as she stood over him, bloody switchblade in hand.

"Really?" She replied.

"Really, so I better make tracks. There's hot coffee in the pot if you're getting up. Just er, take it easy. I'll be back soon."

He then bent down and kissed her on top of her head. Lisa stifled a shudder in reaction. *Fuck*, she thought, *my Father used to do that.*

*

Darren arrived outside an apartment building on a high street in the centre of Hell's Kitchen. An Indian man was standing outside a seven eleven, talking to a female police officer as Darren pulled up to the kerb, parking behind a large coroner's van. He looked to the entrance of the building as Harry exited, coming down a short flight of steps and approached Darren's Sedan.

A couple of teenage black kids were hanging around watching as they drank from soda bottles and smoked. Darren climbed out and met Harry on the sidewalk.

"So what you got for me?"

"Looks the same damn situation, more or less." Harry said and stepped out of earshot of the female officer, walking with Darren.

"Still kinda keeping this on the low key, you understand. But the first victim, she was found with a pentagram, a five-pointed star painted on her upper body. This is the same but so far, we haven't found a murder weapon."

"And the murder weapon on the first victim?"

"What looked to be a kind of ceremonial dagger. But before you ask, we couldn't get one print from it. Now this… well, the case ain't gonna be as open and shut as I'd hoped."

"How'd you get called to this then?"

"The vic' shares the apartment with a guy who works nights. Came home to find his buddy butt-naked in the bedroom. And there's another thing, going by traces of semen and other fluids found on at the scene, there's suggestion his death was post-coital."

"You saying the perp might be a woman?" Darren asked and they came to a standstill by a fire hydrant.

"Difficult to say for sure, unless he likes sticking it in guys. The lab boys will be running tests on the body to see what DNA surfaces."

A slight commotion was then heard. Harry and Darren looked back to the building as a small crowd gathered, just as two coroners brought out a body bag on a stretcher, carefully carrying it down the steps to the awaiting van.

"I was thinking too, that girl Lisa Watts." Harry continued, regaining Darren's attention.

"What about her?"

Origin

"This could mean that her brother's just gone from suspect to potential witness. Why not let her visit him. You never know, her presence might jolt that guy out of slumberland."

Darren pondered the idea as he watched the coroners place the body into the van and slam the doors shut.

Lisa emerged from a shower, dripping wet and wrapped a large towel around her, tucking it securely just above her breasts. Proceeding from the bathroom she went to approach the stairs but paused outside the master bedroom. She hadn't seen inside since she'd arrived and understood Darren never slept there. Curious, Lisa reached for the handle and the door eased open. Venturing into the darkened room, drapes closed by a north facing window, she reached the end of a double bed. Eerily presented on the covers, draped lengthwise like some bizarre keepsake - was a wedding dress.

Walking around to one side she discovered an open photo album on a bedside cabinet. Peering down at it she recognised a slightly younger, happier looking Darren all suited up in a romantic kiss with who she guessed was his wife. She was very pretty. Turning away, Lisa ran her fingers over the beautiful dress. It was just her taste, a Lacey off the shoulder number she could definitely see herself in, if that is, her story was ever likely to have a fairytale ending. Reaching a wardrobe, she pulled the doors open. Inside was completely empty. There were not even any of Darren's clothes. Perhaps much of his things were at the agency?

As she looked around the room again, a couple of observations dawned on her. Darren had at some stage really loved this woman. It was also obvious he was still holding onto the pain that had resulted from her leaving. Maybe he was just as in need of help as she was? Either way, this 'shrine' to their marriage wasn't healthy.

Origin

10

"They will be looking for you now. Although there were no witnesses to the killing, someone saw you leave with him. Choose your next target wisely."

Lisa walked with hands in the pockets of her leather jacket as she headed into the district of Queens. The voice in her head she had to fight not to answer for fear of attracting strange looks from passers by. Lisa had dressed slightly more conservatively, wearing tight leggings, an old t-shirt and those boots she liked with the low heel. She had tied her hair in a ponytail and was wearing sunglasses. As she walked, she handled the switchblade with her fingers, hidden within her pocket, and it was still sticky with Marco's blood.

Pausing outside a tattoo parlour, she looked in through a window. Beyond a lit neon 'open' sign, she observed a skinny guy tattooing a teenage girl's arm, putting the finishing

Craig Micklewright

touches to a sleeve design with various elaborate illustrations. He looked in his early twenties, similar to Lisa's age. In a different life, they may have been friends. However, as she watched him work, memories of that night flooded her mind.

The man was encouraged to undress and get himself hard. Marco held her down, hands planted to her shoulders as she struggled, then felt another guy pull her knickers down her legs. Eventually the skinny guy's erection was probed to her mouth and Marco grinned as she reluctantly took the bulging head between her lips. The sound of whistles and cheers just spurned the skinny guy to defile her face, as hands mauled and someone else penetrated her.

A phone rang out on a wall inside the parlour, and a Chinese girl walked over, lifting the receiver.

"Dragon Flower Tattoo Studio." She answered.

In a room elsewhere in the city, a concerned looking Carlos Equarez stood with a cell phone to his ear, "It's Carlo. Put Travis on."

In the background, standing with a couple of well-built Spanish guys was the young Hispanic girl Marco had exited the club with.

Back at the parlour, the Chinese girl looked around, "Anyone seen Travis?"

"I think he stepped out for a smoke." someone shouted back.

Origin

"He's gone for a smoke, I'll go find him, Sir." The girl said into the phone then placed the receiver on a countertop and walked away.

Carlos sighed, looking back to the girl, "What time was it you saw that girl go off with Marco?"

"It was approaching eleven. He said we were gonna party back at his place, but as soon as he spotted that girl, he…"

"I don't care. This is fucked. We need to find that girl."

He focused on a muted TV fixed to a wall. A reporter was standing across the road from the building in Hell's Kitchen. A banner running across the bottom of the screen read: 'Body of local musician discovered in apartment'. It was accompanied by a publicity photo of Marco holding a guitar.

The Chinese girl emerged from a back door at the rear of the building and looked into a yard, but there was no sign of the skinny kid known as Travis.

As she pulled the door shut again - some distance away down a narrow alley, Lisa rose up as she stood over the body of Travis. She was breathless and held the switchblade in one hand as it dripped blood. On the ground Travis lay with his shirt torn open and a pentagram was scratched into his chest. A deep stab wound sat in the centre. As she stood there looking at her prey, Joseph joined her. A bright yellow tint to her pupils gradually returned to her regular dark brown.

"He deserved it, sis. They violated you in the worst possible way."

Craig Micklewright

Lisa removed a tissue from her pocket and wiped the blood from the blade, stepping over the body and walked on without saying a word.

*

An hour or so later, the alley was closed off with Police tape as Harry Benning reached Travis' corpse, looking down at it in disbelief. A gentle breeze fluttered the bottom of his long trench coat as he was approached by a female detective.

"So if this shit's connected, Sarge, going by the star-thing… we could be looking at a serial killer."

Travis' face had already turned a ghostly white, his eyes bulging in a fixed expression of terror.

"We'll need to find out if they knew one another, could get us one step closer to catching the son-of-a-bitch." Harry responded.

"And still no murder weapon, although the lab came back to say that other guy must have been killed using a knife with a thin blade, perhaps a switchblade, and going by the wound, it had a serrated edge to it." the detective added.

Harry just stared at Travis' face. It didn't seem to matter how long he had been doing this, seeing some dead kid … a kid at least from his perspective, never sat easy.

*

Origin

As it turned afternoon, Darren's Sedan pulled into the carpark of New York State Hospital. As they sat there looking to one entrance, Lisa spoke up.

"I don't see what good this will do, Darren. Joseph is in a coma."

Darren reached over and touched her hand as it lay with the other on her lap, "What if, he saw who did that to your friend? He could be the key to everything. You see that, don't you?"

Lisa just looked to the hospital nervously.

Soon, they both walked down a corridor until they reached a door with a Police officer stationed outside.

"Sorry, folks. No entry."

Darren took out his card, "Darren Maitland. Sergeant Benning said it was alright to drop by."

"Ah yes, and who's this?" the officer asked, staring at Lisa.

"I'm the sister… of the man you got hold up in there." She replied defensively.

The room had a wire-mesh window, and Lisa approached to peer in at Joseph lying in a bed in the centre, wired up to machines. A heart monitor's display showed a steady rhythm. She felt relieved to see him alive and, in the flesh, feeling as though she was being haunted by his ghost otherwise.

The officer looked them both up and down then stepped aside, "Five minutes. Although he's unconscious so you won't get a peep out of him."

Darren smiled, "Thanks officer… Wilson." He said, clocking the officer's badge.

He then approached the door until Lisa stopped him, touching his hand short of him grabbing the doorknob.

"I should see him alone, if that's ok. Why don't you go and get you and me some coffee?" She said and grabbed the doorknob instead, turning it and the door clicked open.

"No problem. I'll be right back." Darren responded, and Lisa applied a kiss to his cheek before entering the room and closing the door behind her.

Inside, Lisa looked apprehensively to the bed, but as she laid eyes on her brother, his face expressionless, tubes fixed to his nostrils and a bleep-bleep coming from the machine – her heart went out to him. She sat down in a chair beside the bed and quickly took Joseph's hand in her own, holding it up from the bed.

"Hey there, little brother." She said quietly, "I don't know if you're able to hear me, but if recent events are anything to go by, I think you just might."

She sighed, bowing her head and rested her forehead against his hand, "I'm doing as you asked, brother... I've done as you've asked. Things I never thought possible."

She opened her eyes and looked at him again, "Since this started, I've been feeling different. There's a rage developing inside me and I think I know what it is. It's the demon. That thing... and I'm scared it's taking over. I must finish this, or I could lose who I am as well as lose you. And I can't lose you, Joseph. You're my brother... my everything."

Tears welled up in her eyes. She sniffed her nose and let go of his hand, "Tonight though... I've got ideas. Tonight, I

Origin

will be almost done. Then, it'll be over, and we can go away, leave this God forsaken city and disappear."

She lay her head down on his arm, his warmth soothing as a tear escaped to pool in the corner of her eye before rolling off her nose. She closed her eyes, wallowing in the moment. She then felt a movement, and jolted, sitting up and gasped to see the black cloaked figure lying in the bed in place of Joseph. His face was hooded, but his Bovine features protruded out.

"You are getting stronger. You will need to be strong to complete your work. I have much faith in you, child."

Lisa bolted upright, staggering away as the chair toppled over, making a loud clatter as it hit the floor.

"Where's Joseph? Where has he gone?" She cried out.

"He is here, I have just taken his body, like I can take yours. Together we will turn light into darkness."

"What does that mean?"

"Not for you to concern yourself with, my child. Freeing your brother and yourself, that is all you need to be thinking of."

Lisa turned and rushed to the door. She burst out of the room, colliding with the Police officer as she did so.

"Hey, lady – are you ok?" He asked.

Lisa was panting and looked back to the open door, to see her brother once again lying motionless in the bed. She shoved past the officer and hurried down the corridor, passing Darren as he returned carrying two plastic cups of coffee.

"Lisa? What is it?"

"Let's just go." She replied as she walked away.

Darren stood still, looking to her then to the officer, who appeared equally confused.

Origin

11

Darren pulled up to the kerb and turned to Lisa as she held a near-empty coffee in one hand.

"You know you can talk to me, don't you Lisa?" He said.

Staring into the black shallow depths of the coffee, Lisa sighed and nodded.

"He didn't say anything then?" Darren continued.

She shook her head, looking to the door.

"What got you so scared?"

"I'd rather not talk about it." She replied quietly.

Darren exhaled slowly, reluctant to push any further, "Ok, er… you alright me dropping you back here, I need to go over to the agency and grab some stuff."

Lisa then opened her door, presented with the driveway to Darren's house.

Craig Micklewright

Climbing out, the door swung shut and she went to walk away until Darren called after her.

"Lisa… er, you gonna be alright, hun?"

She glanced back and nodded, appreciating his concern even if matters were now too far gone to see Darren as anything other than a good friend. The deluded idea that he could ever be her saviour, was now dead in the water.

"Maybe I'll take a nap." She replied and Darren smiled to her before adjusting the gears and driving off down the road.

Lisa proceeded up the driveway, taking out a key and let herself in through the front door.

As Darren drove, he took out his cell phone from his jacket's inside pocket to re-read a message he'd received from Harry.

'Darren, there's been another development. I've dropped off some items at your agency. Speak to you soon. Don't say anything to Miss Watts.'

Darren tapped his reply with his thumb: 'I'm heading over there now.' - then pressed send. Concealing the phone again, he trod down on the accelerator.

Darren arrived outside Blue Circle Detective Agency a short while later. Exiting his car, it had begun to rain, the late afternoon sun becoming obscured by the developing dark clouds. Letting himself into the front office, he was immediately met with a Manila envelope on his welcome mat.

Tearing it open, he kicked the door shut and walked around the reception desk to his back office. Inside he sat down behind a desk and emptied the contents of the

Origin

envelope before him. Several crime scene photos were presented, along with a sticky note which read 'And now we have three. Are we looking at a serial killer?'.

Darren sighed, and picked up the photos, perusing them individually. He clasped eyes on Tina, tied to a blood-stained bed, semi-naked and with the pentagram painted across her breasts. He recalled eyeing her up a few times when he'd driven by the district on those particularly lonely nights. He had never stopped for her though. Hey, one does not usually shit in one's own back yard, so to say, but if he was ever in the mood to pay for sex, like he often had been in recent times, it was usually outside of Springdale. Lisa however, was to catch his attention in a way that Tina's more stereotypical 'blonde bombshell' looks had not. Perhaps if he had chosen Tina that night, Lisa would be the one he was looking at in the photo. The thought made him shudder, all too aware of the feelings towards her that had been developing since they met.

Switching to the next photo, it showed a naked Marco. He wasn't familiar with the man. As he turned to the final photo, like Harry he too was taken back by how young the skinny guy looked. This time the pentagram appeared to be carved into his flesh. *This is horrific,* he thought.

Darren placed the photos face down on his desk, then noticed a fourth. Picking it up he saw it was a stock photo of a switchblade. Turning it over he discovered that Harry had written on the other side.

'Forensics are saying the two most recent murders were done with a knife very much like this. Any thoughts?'

Darren flipped the photo over and studied the image again. For the briefest of moments, he visualised Lisa handling a similar, rather scary-looking knife at Tina's apartment. *Coincidence, surely!* He told himself.

*

The rain barely let up for the remainder of the day and was pouring heavily as a black BMW splashed a puddle, coming to a halt outside the apartment building in Springdale. Lisa sat alongside a black guy who was wearing a tailored suit. Apparently, he ran his own successful business; something about online currency. She'd changed into her usual attire of leather mini skirt, heels along with a t-shirt and her leather jacket, although her legs were bare.

"We should do this again sometime." He said, offering her a rolled-up wad of bills.

Lisa, thick red lipstick coating her lips, black eyeliner accentuating her brown eyes, returned a smile as she took the cash.

"Maybe. I'm here most nights. Thanks for a pleasant evening." She responded and climbed out.

The car pulled away as she took shelter by the building and checked the money. She then rolled it back up and stuffed it into her jacket. Around half an hour passed until another car appeared, and as predicted she recognised Carlos at the wheel of his white Jag, doing his rounds.

"Lisa?" He called.

Origin

Under the glow of a second-floor window, Lisa pushed away from the building and slowly approached the car. The rain had begun to calm, now just spots that bounced off the leather of her jacket.

She reached the passenger side and leaned her elbows on the door, peering in.

"I got your money if that's why you're here." She said.

"That and well, perhaps we need to talk. Jump in."

Lisa faked disinterest, trying to appear like seeing her pimp was no biggie, and not at all part of her Devine plan. She opened the door and climbed in, Carlos immediately treading down on the accelerator, kicking up water as the Jag sped off down the street.

As he drove, Carlos inhaled loudly, "Hey babe, you wearing panties or am I getting pussy smell mixed up with cum stench?"

"Er, I use rubbers, doofus." Lisa answered.

Carlos smirked, "Watch your mouth, sweetheart or I might have a barrel with your name on it."

Lisa stifled a laugh and looked out of the window, "So what we gonna talk about?"

"You seen Marco lately?"

Lisa already knew where this was going, "Why? I heard someone finally offed that sleazy bastard."

The Jag suddenly screeched to a stop and Lisa almost hit her head on the dash. Passing car horns sounded.

"The fuck, Carlos? I could've ended up on the tarmac!"

Carlo suddenly pointed a gun at her, "Listen up you fuckin' whore. I already know you were the last to see Marco

180

alive, and now a little buddy tells me young Travis was found with a damn star carved into his chest. Both were there the other night, right? Who's next huh? You looking to come after me, you psycho bitch?"

Lisa looked at him then burst out laughing. Carlos stared at her incensed. As she started to compose herself, she exhaled and stared at him.

"Seriously, Carlos? You think I killed Marco? Me?? He's twice the fuckin' size of me. I was bullied in high school. I ain't ever been in a fight that I've won. I'm a fuckin' coward. Jeez. We gonna go somewhere and fuck? Because if not let me out, 'cause I've got money to earn. Or we gonna sit here until my coos is too dried up to pay for?"

Carlos gradually lowered the gun, and bashed the steering wheel with his fist, "Fuck! What's going on!? Is this the same creep who killed Tina?"

Lisa focused on him, still aware of the gun, "Tina?" She repeated.

"Like that wasn't going to get back to me? I owned that girl's ass. If she farted, I was the first to hear about it. They say your brother did it after strangling his girl?"

The jungle drums seemed alive and well in this city, Lisa mused.

"Welcome to my world, Carlos. Your fuckin' guess is as good as mine."

Carlos slowly smiled, "Ok, ok... let's go back to my place. Maybe I owe you an apology. Hey, we could share that bottle of Rioja I've been waiting for an excuse to cork."

He adjusted the gear stick then applied the accelerator again, and Lisa jolted back in her seat as the Jag continued down the street.

Origin

*

Darren awoke on his couch back at the house. The TV was the only flickering light in the room, the sound low, with some long-haired rock band playing on the screen. He wasn't sure how long he'd been out, although the bottle of whisky on the coffee table was a contributing factor. Next to the bottle sat his wallet, along with his removed wedding ring, an item that had begun to grow heavier since Lisa had remarked on it.

Eventually he reached the upstairs hallway and paused outside the spare room. Raising one hand he knocked twice, unsure if Lisa was still home.

"Lisa?" He called, then grabbed the doorknob.

Easing the door open, he was presented with a neatly made bed, moonlight beaming in from the window, and no sign of Lisa. He didn't really need to guess where she would be. Working the streets it seemed, was in her blood.

"Goddammit, Lisa." He remarked fearing the worst.

If there was in fact a serial killer out there, a girl in her profession would be easy pickings. He turned on his heals, storming back out.

Hurrying down the stairs, he snatched his jacket off the stand, causing it to wobble, then left through his front door. With the door slamming in his wake, Darren approached his car parked on the driveway, putting on his jacket in the process, then climbed in.

12

Carlos walked around Lisa as she stood in the living area at his studio apartment. She had been instructed to strip down to her black lingerie and high heels and he was inspecting her body like a critic might inspect a work of art. Demonic intervention or not, she was in the best shape of her life.

Lisa could feel a heat on her bare legs from an open log fireplace, its dancing flames creating a flickering glow throughout the room.

Carlos stepped before her, and ran a hand up her thigh, over the waistband of her knickers, across her ribs, then palmed her right breast, squeezing and needing the flesh. He ran his thumb over the soft material, feeling the prominence of a nipple and Lisa let out a gasp.

"You know, you're exquisite. Such soft flesh. You're going to be my number one girl from now on. Such beauty

Origin

will make us both a lot of money. You should be excited. Why are you not smiling?"

Lisa's eyes, which had been transfixed on an area behind Carlos, slowly turned to him, and her lips curved into a smile.

His hand ran back down her body and this time he cupped her between her legs, his fingers rubbing at her Lacey crotch. She bit her lip, playing along and just as he delved his hand into her knickers, Lisa turned her head to see a rather large bottle of wine floating a few feet from Carlos' head.

"That's right sweetheart, you're ready for me, aren't you? I promise I'll be gentle." He said, and as a finger probed inside her - the bottle suddenly flew and shattered against his head.

She staggered away to avoid glass fragments and splash of wine, just as Carlos collapsed unconscious.

"Yeah, now I'm ready for you." She remarked, looking down at him before walking over to where her clothes lay, piled neatly on the arm of a couch.

Grabbing her jacket where the roll of money protruded from the inside pocket, she retrieved the switchblade ... and as she glanced back to Carlos, her eyes changed to a bright yellow, like a switch had been flicked on.

Darren slowed his Sedan as he attracted the attention of a couple of hookers. A black woman walked over to the passenger side and peered in at him.

"You looking to party, Mr?" She asked.

He grinned back. She was a pretty one and had large breasts that under different circumstances he'd have loved to bury his face within.

"No no, honey. I'm looking for someone. Her name's Lisa, about your height, dark hair... occasionally works these streets."

The woman stood upright as her friend came over, a young-looking redhead.

"Sounds familiar. She hangs around with some blonde girl?"

"Yeah." Darren confirmed.

"Didn't she go off with Carlos?" The other woman piped up.

"Who's Carlos?"

The black woman saw another car pull up and a small, Korean looking hooker approached it.

"You not 5-Oh, are ya?"

Darren shook his head, "I swear. You girls are safe. I just really need to find her."

The black woman sighed, "He's our pimp. Lives up in the Bronx, Mr... but you ain't heard that from me. Drives a white Jaguar."

"That's a lot of help. Thanks." Darren responded.

The Sedan then drove on as the two hookers continued to ply their trade.

*

Lisa sat on her knees. A thick coating of blood smeared her upper body, making her breasts as they bulged out of her bra, shimmer a deep crimson. Sitting all nonchalant, she raised a glistening liver to her mouth and bit into it, fluid

Origin

squirting as she casually ate. As she swallowed, she ran her tongue over rose-red lips then applied blood-stained fingers to her mouth, proceeding to lick them clean. *Damn it tasted good.* Laid out beside her was Carlos. His chest had been ripped open and his ribcage jutted out like the jaws of a Venus fly trap. Internal organs were displayed, his intestines having spilled out as a slight steam lingered in the air. Lisa was coated with his blood, her thighs, her arms, some parts of her face as well as her underwear. She continued to suck leisurely on her finger as her glowing yellow pupils slowly returned to brown, and then - she spotted her reflection in the surface of a large TV, seeing herself, seeing the blood.

Falling back in horror, she looked to Carlos and let out a shriek. Had she done this?? Scrambling to her feet, Lisa backed off in her stilettos to reveal that Carlos' body lay in the centre of a large pentagram, painted in his blood on the wood flooring. Turning away from the grisly sight, she grabbed her jacket, pulling it on before making for the door. This could not be happening! She told herself repeatedly. She had to wake up from this nightmare!

Lisa came hurtling from the apartment, holding her jacket shut with one hand, colliding with the facing wall and leaving smears of blood. She reached a stairwell and thrust herself against the door, escaping inside just as a young couple came into the corridor. They halted in their tracks as they noticed the blood.

*

Minutes later, Darren was driving slowly down a street in the heart of The Bronx. He wasn't sure what he was doing in all truth, but the myriad of fears and uncertainty plaguing his mind felt like they would only be eased with the knowledge of Lisa's safety.

As he continued out of the main high street towards the more built-up suburbs and housing blocks, his headlights caught a figure staggering in and out of the road, walking rather drunkenly. As he drew closer, his eyes widened in disbelief as he recognised Lisa, walking towards the car. He slowed to a halt just as she fell against the car's bonnet. Quickly he climbed out, rushing over and then noticed the blood and her state of undress. He grabbed her and she looked to him as he took her in his arms, and she collapsed against him. History would repeat this encounter almost exact, a different place, a different woman, years later … little did he know at the time.

"Lisa! It's me! What happened?"

Lisa lifted her head to look at him again, more blood staining her face … she appeared catatonic.

"Come on, let's get you home." He added, walking her around to the passenger side, opening the door and helped her into the car.

Sitting alongside her, he paused from driving as he pondered the situation. Again, he saw her handling that knife. *No… surely not.* He looked to her as she lay slumped in the passenger seat, slightly breathless, her chest heaving beneath the jacket. Blood stained his seat and the surrounding

Origin

upholstery. He began to hate the thoughts swirling around in his head.

"Who did this to you? Lisa…" He said quietly, as if scared of the answer.

She murmured like she was only semi-conscious, then said: "It's ok, it's not my blood… just, just drive."

Darren adjusted the gear stick then trod down on the accelerator and headed into the night.

A cell phone buzzed on a bedside cabinet. A shape moved under the covers, then a hand reached out to grab the phone, flipping it open as Harry's head peeked out from a blanket.

"Sergeant Benning." He said groggily.

"Sir, there's been another one." came a voice, and Harry immediately sat up, covers falling away to reveal pyjamas.

"Seriously? When?"

"Hard to tell at this stage. A body was found and well, it's bad… real fucking bad."

Harry ran his other hand over his face as he turned, dropping his feet into a pair of slippers, then got up, walking towards where his bedroom door stood ajar.

"Ok, send me the details. I'm on my way." He responded, then ended the call walking whilst mumbling to himself as he left his room.

*

Afterwards, Darren stood on the upstairs hallway of his house, looking and feeling distressed. He knocked on the door to the bathroom and was able to hear water running.

Inside, Lisa, wearing a bathrobe, stood before a wash basin as she wiped the remnants of blood from her face, then gave it another douse of water before examining her reflection.

"Lisa? You ok in there? Er... I think we need to talk..." came Darren's voice.

Lisa sighed, feeling hopeless. How could she explain? She could barely explain it to herself.

"I'll be out in a minute." She shouted back.

Darren walked away, heading back downstairs, understanding that Lisa might need some space, at least for now.

Lisa turned off the faucet, grabbing a towel from a rail and dried her face. She then looked back to the mirror and gasped at seeing the cloaked demon behind her, it's face steeped in shadow within its hood.

"You have pleased me." Its voice rumbled, "But you are not yet done."

Lisa looked around, concerned that Darren may have heard the creature's words.

"I... I can't do this anymore." She said in a semi-whisper.

The demon approached as she looked to its reflection.

"Then I will choose for you. Your next victim is here in this house. Complete the circle, child and your brother will suffer no more. Choose to defy me and the both of you will be damned for eternity."

Origin

Lisa stared at the creature, "No, please... you said it would be someone who has hurt me. Not him. He's helped me, not hurt me. No, not Darren."

"It is too late for sentiment. He has been chosen. Time is running out. He must die tonight."

Lisa gripped the wash basin and closed her eyes tight, gritting her teeth. After a moment she let out a gasp.

"I can't... I won't!" She retorted, raising her voice.

"There is no alternative. You are my vessel now, and you have a task to complete."

She shook her head, then ran one hand along the porcelain of the wash basin to a shelf, and grasped a straight razor as it sat next to an electric toothbrush. She opened her eyes wide and focused on the demon.

"This vessel... will be useless to you dead!" She snapped, suddenly running the blade down her wrist, and cried out as a thick red gush was released.

"Foolish girl." The demon said and faded away just as Lisa repeated the action on her other wrist, crying in despair as blood splashed the wash basin copiously and she had to steady herself against it, a dizziness washing over her.

Down in the kitchen, Darren was opening a pack of ground coffee when he suddenly heard a loud thud. Dropping the coffee, its contents spilling across the tiled floor, he hurried out of the kitchen, instantly sprinting up the stairs. Reaching the bathroom, he tried the handle. The door was locked.

"Lisa? Lisa! What was that noise just now?"

No answer.

190

He stepped away from the door then suddenly kicked it open, splitting the doorframe and it swung open to reveal Lisa lying on the floor as blood formed a pool around her.

Horrified, he rushed in and dropped to his knees, grabbing her and pulling her into his arms, "Lisa! Fuck... Lisa! What have you done?! Goddammit, stay with me sweetheart!"

Origin

13

Harry stood holding a scented cloth over his mouth and nose. Having arrived at Carlos' apartment, he looked down at the pimp's remains as Police officers and coroners busied themselves around him. He had seen some things during his long career, but this was one for the books.

"Sergeant… we found this." A young female officer said, and he looked to her as she held up a transparent bag housing a blood-soaked switchblade.

"Ok, put it in evidence, Somerset. But whatever did this… used more than a knife. It's like he was torn open like a piece of meat."

He walked out into the corridor, where more crimson stains formed a trail across the floor towards the stairwell door. The young couple who had been there before were also being interviewed in the background.

"What you make of this?" He asked a black female officer.

"Could be the perp. These footprints look like they were wearing heels. Backs up your theory that we could be looking for a female, or at the very least, a cross dresser."

Harry nodded then walked away, taking out his cell and scrolled through his contacts until he landed on Darren's name. He made a call.

In a hospital emergency department meanwhile, Darren stood outside one of the cubicles as he answered his phone, "Harry. This isn't a good time, what is it?" He asked, his face flushed like he'd been crying.

"It's bad, Darren. A fourth victim, a guy we've suspected as being a local pimp and well, it's savage. We gotta find this psycho."

"I'm at the hospital, er… Brooklyn Hospital. It's Lisa. She er… tried to kill herself."

"What? Why?"

Darren recalls the hooker informing him that Lisa had got into the car of their pimp … *was it the same guy Harry was referring to?*

"I don't know. It's messing me up, Harry. I can't handle this. I'm scared that…"

"That what?"

"That it's her, Harry… that she's who we're looking for."

"You can't be serious."

Origin

"This may have started with her brother, but these last few murders… I wish I wasn't thinking this but… I found her Harry and she was… she was covered in blood. And I mean covered."

A tear rolled down his cheek as he spoke all his fears out loud.

Harry reached the end of the corridor, looking distraught, "Found her where?" He asked.

"The Bronx."

A shiver ran down Harry's spine like an icicle against his skin, "Alright. I'll get a car over to you. Where is she, right this minute?"

"She slashed her wrists, Harry. I think maybe, she couldn't handle what she was doing. She must have had her reasons - this isn't her."

"Well if your hunch is right, your hooker friend's a killer, Darren and therefore she must be detained. If you saw this guy here, believe me you'd understand."

Darren looked back to the cubical, a blue curtain concealing any view of the inside, "I know Harry. For her own sake she must be stopped. They got her in the E.R… I don't know yet if she's gonna make it."

*

About an hour later, Lisa had been moved to a room and was in a stable condition. Police had been placed outside in the corridor, and she had been secured to the bed with straps on her arms. She lay in a bed with an oxygen mask over her face and bandages were wrapped around both wrists. It was a miracle she was even alive, the doctors had reported, from the amount of blood she'd lost. Yet something was still not done with her.

Opening her eyes, she moved gradually, until she discovered her bonds. Moaning softly, she raised her head from the pillow to discover Joseph sitting at the end of the mattress.

"Welcome back, sis." He said with a grin.

"Where am I?" Her slightly muffled voice remarked.

"Hospital. Yeah, there's no getting out of this, I'm afraid. Your work's not finished." Joseph replied.

Lisa closed her eyes with distress. Suddenly, they sprang back open, pupils bright yellow. She tugged at the straps holding her to the rails either side of the bed, then with force, they broke away.

Lisa's body levitated into the air, the bedsheet falling away as the mask was pulled from her face, just as the gown they'd dressed her in shredded itself like it was made of tissue paper. Floating naked, high above the bed, she started to jolt and shake as cuts appeared across her flesh, and gradually a pentagram formed, carving into her body over her breasts and abdomen.

Outside the room a police officer was alerted to a loud crash. Immediately he turned and applied a key to the door just as another officer returned carrying a plastic cup of coffee.

Origin

"What was that noise?" He enquired.

The first officer unlocked the door, "Dunno. Stay back." He said, and opened the door as he took a revolver from his belt. Walking inside, he discovered the bed turned onto its side. A heart machine lay sparking. Looking around he then saw a screen, and spotted a silhouette of a figure behind.

"Step out! Now!" He shouted, pointing the gun.

"Oh, officer, put that away, I just want to play." came Lisa's voice, it's tone childlike.

The officer walked around the upturned bed towards the screen. He then shoved the screen aside to reveal - nobody.

Suddenly, Lisa appeared behind him, eyes glowing.

The other officer approached the door, but staggered away as his colleague slammed against the wall of the corridor with enough force to crack the plaster. Shocked, the officer dropped his coffee, and went to retrieve his own gun just as Lisa walked out and slowly turned, her body covered in streaks of blood as the carved pentagram bled profusely. Before the officer could pull out his gun however, she raised her hand, and an invisible force propelled him off his feet. He hit the floor and went sliding down the corridor, crashing into a vending machine the other end.

Glancing to the concussed officer by the wall, Lisa walked on, glowing eyes illuminating the corridor around her.

Darren left a cafeteria on the ground floor just as Harry entered the E.R. meeting up with several other officers.

"So is the suspect secure?" Harry asked.

"No worries, Sarge, we have her on the third floor away from the other patients and there's a Police detail outside her room. So, we sure this is the perp?" A large black officer responded.

Darren then joined them, a few patients sitting around the waiting area.

"Nothing's guaranteed yet, Jackson, but yeah it looks that way." He replied before Harry could say anything.

Harry shot a look to him, "Er yeah, thanks Maitland but, this is our situation now, why don't you get yourself home?"

Darren focused on Harry, "Really, Harry? I bought you this. I fuckin 'betrayed her, that shit'll haunt me, but it's like you said, if she did this, she had to be stopped."

They were then alerted to a male nurse as he came out from a reception desk looking concerned.

"Er, officers… we might have a problem. An alarm has been raised on the third floor. That's where they're keeping that woman, right? It's an amber light. Nobody ever presses the amber alarm!"

Harry and Darren looked at one another.

"Lisa." Darren said.

Lisa was discarding hospital staff, security guards and orderlies like they were nothing. One doctor was thrown through a window to plummet to a car park below. Police entered a corridor aiming their guns until they were pulled from their hands without discharging… nothing it seemed, could stop her.

Origin

As one nurse ran into a stairwell, she screamed and fell to her death as a force tipped her over a railing, and Lisa entered behind her, then gradually ascended the steps.

Harry and Darren, along with several officers exited an elevator on the same floor, meeting up with the one officer who had been thrown against the wall. He was nursing a nasty-looking cut to his head, clearly shaken.

"Where is she??" Darren said with desperation.

"Who?" The officer asked, feeling dazed.

"Lisa Watts. Now focus, which way did she go?" Harry asked.

The officer leaned against the wall, "She entered a stairwell… there's a fire escape just back this way." He replied then turned to head back the way he came.

"Ok, get some guys to cut her off on the floors below. Darren you're with me. She might be making for the roof. If she is, there'll be nowhere left for her to run. Back up should be on its way."

Darren revealed his own pistol as Harry hurried onward. If she escaped, there was a clear chance it would not end well. He had to reach her. He had to try and get through to her before it was too late.

On the flat rooftop of Brooklyn Hospital, Lisa walked as rain fell heavily, partially washing the blood from her body. Treading puddles with her bare feet and with the glow of her eyes lighting the area around her, she soon reached the end of the roof. Slightly breathless, she looked out across the vast city rooftops, distant skyscrapers on the horizon, the clouds rumbling as lightening flashed in the sky.

After a moment, a voice pierced the night, and she jolted before looking over her shoulder.

"Lisa! Stop!" Darren shouted, several metres behind, aiming his pistol as Harry stood beside him doing the same.

"I'll handle this, Darren." Harry said and went to step forward until Darren yanked him back.

"No, Harry… I have to do this." He said, then walked a few steps forward as Lisa turned to face him, inches from the edge of the roof – *my God, what's happened to you?* He thought.

A helicopter flew into position overhead, as an officer inside talked to Harry via a microphone, "We have eyes on the target, Sarge'. Just say the word."

Another officer onboard was aiming a rifle with a scope attached as the helicopter hovered high above the hospital.

On the roof, Harry held up a CB radio, "Hold your fire." He said back as he watched Darren aiming at Lisa.

With her glowing eyes and grisly appearance, Harry could hardly comprehend what he was witnessing. Lisa observed the both of them with a strange curiosity.

"This isn't you, Lisa. I know you're in there. It's me, Darren, remember? Come on, it's over… Stop this, please." Darren shouted.

A clap of thunder felt like it shook the whole building. This was no regular storm. Darren stepped forward, and as he did so, Lisa backed off onto the ledge. A steep drop was all that remained between her and the street below. A strong

Origin

wind blew her long black hair and the harsh rain seemed to graze her skin. *She looks cold*, Darren observed as he gradually lowered his gun, instead raising a hand to beckon her to him.

"Come away from the edge, Lisa, I'm begging you. Don't end it like this. I'm here, I'll protect you, nobody will ever harm you again."

As Lisa noticed tears in his eyes, the glow of her own dimmed. He was having an effect, Harry observed, his words were working.

Gradually her pupils returned to brown, and she gasped as if awakened.

"Darren?" She responded.

Darren stepped closer, and Lisa glanced back to the drop, vertigo suddenly hitting her. She looked to Darren again, eyes wide and full of anguish.

"You can't help me!" She blurted, "It won't ever leave me. There's only one way out for me now."

"What are you talking about, Lisa?"

The helicopter hovering overhead suddenly lit her up with a searchlight. Harry backed off, shouting into his radio.

"Stand down. We got this!"

The helicopter remained overhead, the officer aiming the rifle, a finger poised on the trigger.

"Whilst I exist, it will never give up. You gotta do it, Darren… you gotta kill me." Lisa shouted.

Darren didn't want to hear such words, but something deep within him told him she was right… whatever it was, would never leave her. It had a hold on her like a vice.

"No… give yourself up, it doesn't need to be this way. Please, Lisa." He exclaimed as tears mixed with the rainfall that soaked his face.

Lisa then focused on him and held her hand out as if to stop his approach. Harry went to aim his gun but hesitated as he saw Darren aim his again. However this time his hand was shaking, like he wasn't in control.

"No, Lisa… don't!" Darren shouted, struggling.

Then as she held her hand out towards him, Lisa's eyes began to glow again just as her fingers gestured back like she was pulling the trigger on an invisible gun … forcing Darren's gun to discharge.

He screamed out as a bullet penetrated her chest, the impact knocking her back and she tipped backwards off the roof. Immediately, Darren ran to the ledge as Harry joined him. They dropped to their knees, looking to the street below to discover, to Darren's continued horror, Lisa impaled on wrought-iron fencing. She gave a final, agonizing gasp, before going limp, eyes wide and motionless as death took her in its cold, merciless grasp.

Harry pulled Darren away, embracing him and he cried out his pain against Harry's chest, the searchlight illuminated them as rain pelting down. That night - they were both changed.

Origin

PART THREE

204

Craig Micklewright

1

Miami

2014

Patricia Willis exited an on-suite bathroom at Jackson Memorial Hospital, re-entering her room as the sound of the toilet flushing echoed in her wake. Wearing a thin gown and with her head bandaged where her hair had been shaved, she slowly climbed into bed just as the door to her room opened.

"Ah, Miss Willis you have a visitor." A young nurse said.

"Who is it, Suzy?" Patricia said back.

"Some detective. Says he's a friend."

Patricia instantly knew who the nurse was referring to, "Oh right, ok, let him in. Thanks Suzy."

The nurse disappeared as Patricia sat herself upright with two large pillows supporting her. She didn't need to be in bed,

Origin

but the surprisingly comfortable mattress over the past few days had moulded itself so perfectly to her, she preferred it to the hard, upright armchair situated nearby. After a brief silence, the door opened again, and Detective Jim Davenport walked in. She found herself delighted to see him.

"Patricia! I hope you don't mind me dropping by." He said, wearing a long over coat, and came to sit in the rigid chair.

A large vase of flowers stood pride of place on a table by the wall next to an I.V. drip that wasn't currently in use.

"So, what do I owe this visit, Detective?" Patricia asked, much of the swelling and bruising on her face having reduced in the time she had been there.

"Call me Jim. I wanted to drop by earlier in the week, but well, I'm here now and, I was shocked when news broke you'd been attacked. I'm er, sure you've already answered all the questions, but did you really not see who did this to you?"

Patricia narrowed her eyes knowing that giving away any details to the Police was likely to destroy her own, currently stalled investigation, if that is, *the sect* hadn't already been spooked.

"Er no, I was grabbed from behind. Next thing I knew I woke up in here. You know, I got back from theatre yesterday morning. There was some swelling to my brain apparently. S'pose I'm lucky to be alive."

"I want to help you Patricia, but there are no leads, and I haven't been able to get in touch with your friend, Mr Thomas."

Patricia immediately felt concerned. She knew Blake had been upset by the attack, it had affected him as she knew it would, but he wouldn't just shoot off, would he? It suddenly dawned on her that he was also the only person, other than her assailant, to know who had actually done this.

She scanned the detective's serious expression with her eyes, "What do you mean? Hasn't he been at the agency? Have you tried his cell?"

"Nobody has seen or heard from him in the past forty eight hours."

Just then, a doctor poked his head around the door and knocked twice, "Sorry to disturb you, Miss Willis, but that test is back. You requested we bring the results to you straight away."

Patricia glanced from the detective to the doctor and nodded, "It's fine."

The doctor entered holding a clipboard and came to the foot of the bed as Davenport looked at him inquisitively.

"The results of your pregnancy test show that yes indeed, you are expecting. Congratulations."

Davenport shot a look to Patricia with surprise.

"Oh, Patricia…"

"Thank you, doctor." She responded and the doctor hurried away as she bowed her head, looking at her hands, a hospital identity band around her wrist. She was both relieved and apprehensive.

"Oh, er… not good news? Did you have any idea?" Davenport said.

"It's not that… it's just, bittersweet. The father, it was David Henderson. Shit, I barely knew him."

Origin

"The owner of the detective agency? I see. Damn, I'm so sorry Patricia."

"Don't be." Patricia continued and raised her head, looking to Davenport, "What's done is done. Time to move on and first things first, it's time I got myself out of here."

"Hey, don't rush yourself. You're recovering from an operation, right? I've got this. Let me help, Patricia."

He reached forward, touching her arm. The contact of his fingers on her skin made the light hairs react. Patricia looked to his hand then back to his face. He was a good friend, she realised - but she couldn't involve him. At least not yet.

"No, you're right. I've got to heal first." She replied with a smile, even if she had no intentions of lingering in the small hospital room, not whilst Blake was AWOL and not whilst her investigation was still on-going.

*

As night drew in, Patricia pulled on a pair of hospital-issued pyjama bottoms. Standing in the bathroom she fastened the buttons on her blouse. A few blood stains discoloured the collar, but she hadn't managed to procure anything from the apartment, a situation not helped by Blake's absence. Checking her reflection, she noticed some strands of hair that hung over the bandage wrapped around her scalp, showing that thankfully, she hadn't been balded. She knew she wasn't 100% yet and some pain still lingered, causing her to wonder if a migraine was imminent – but she needed to track down Blake. Hopefully he hadn't gone and done something stupid. Slipping her feet into a pair of

Craig Micklewright

hospital-issue Crocs, she ventured back into her room, grabbing a handbag on the way, then made for the door.

Patricia exited the hospital mostly unnoticed minutes later. A light rainfall was coming down and a few overhanging palm trees swayed in the wind. Feeling vulnerable she headed down a path towards an expansive car park and proceeded towards the street, in hope of maybe hailing a cab.

She managed to get on a passing bus and went and sat down, looking out of the window to watch the city lights scroll by. A strange looking old man seemed to leer at her but she chose not to react. With her handbag on her lap, she opened the clasp and retrieved her cell, scrolling through the names before landing on Blake. She made a call and placed the cell to her ear, hoping but not confident that he would pick up. It rang for a few seconds, then went to voice mail.

"Blake. It's me. Where the hell are you? If you get this, call me back. I've sort of discharged myself from the hospital."

She lowered the phone, feeling helpless and increasingly worried.

After a while she ascended the steps of the apartment building and reached the fifth floor, pushing the stairwell door open and proceeded into a corridor. Reaching Blake's door, she applied a key to the lock and gained entry. As she walked in, she was presented with abject silence. Nudging the door shut again she wandered into the kitchen, looking around as she placed her bag on a counter top. She took her

Origin

cell phone out as she noticed the hob was immaculate, unused. There were no dishes in the sink either.

Walking into the living area, the drapes were closed, and she switched on a tall lamp by the sofa - immediately presented with an untidy coffee table; a mass of paperwork she quickly recognised from the agency. It was all the work she'd gathered about The Sect of the Fallen Angel. Patricia sighed, foolish to think Blake would leave it alone considering what had happened. The passion for the job may have passed to her in recent months, but that passion had been his to start with.

She tried his number again, and as she applied her cell to her ear, she began to hear a distant melody play. Recognising it, she walked into a hallway and followed the noise until she reached Blake's bedroom door. Pausing before she grasped the handle, a horrible thought occurred to her - *what if he was in here. What if he was dead?*

Like ripping off a band-aid she opened the door wide to feast her eyes on: an unmade bed and Blake's cell phone ringing and vibrating across the mattress. Darting her eyes around the room she was relieved to not find his corpse. Instantly, she pocketed her own cell and grabbed his, flipping it open to answer as it rang off and went to voice mail. She ended the call and realised the phone was unlocked, Blake obviously not a stickler for security. Curious, she hovered her thumb over the displayed apps, then felt drawn to the photos, to reveal a series of pictures. Opening each one in turn, she discovered various candid shots of none other than her attacker, Lucas Black - leaving the building of the sect, getting in a car, and arriving at another location in the suburbs.

Craig Micklewright

She closed her eyes as she felt herself violently thrown into a vision; receiving blow after blow as that man's bearded face leered down at her with hatred in his eyes. Gasping she opened her eyes again, noticing how her hand was shaking.

"Oh God…" She breathed, "Where are you, Blake?"

*

A cab arrived on a street in the heart of the city and Patricia climbed out, thanking the driver as she did so then placed her purse back in her bag, hanging the bag over her shoulder by its strap. Wearing a fresh t-shirt and Levi's, sneakers on her feet, she looked across the road. She knew it wasn't exactly wise to be anywhere near these people, but as she laid her eyes on the Sect's three-story building, she was shocked to discover a blackened, burnt-out husk like there had recently been a blazing fire. The windows were boarded up and a large metal chain secured the front door. She hurried across the road, avoiding traffic until she stood outside in view of a partially melted security camera. *Jesus Christ, what is going on?* She asked herself.

Walking around to a side alley, she cautiously stepped through some brambles and over discarded beer cans before reaching a rickety-looking fire escape. Looking skyward, she noticed an open window. She didn't hesitate, eager to find any clue to go on. If these people were willing to beat her up, there was no reason they'd get frightened off so easily. With determination and a renewed energy she hadn't anticipated, Patricia began to ascend the wrought iron ladder.

Origin

Pulling a sash window open fully, she poked a leg in, feeling with her foot for the floor then climbed into a darkened room. A smell of burnt wood and stale dust particles filled her lungs and she coughed as she stood up straight. Reaching to her handbag, she retrieved a small pistol, which glinted in the moonlight from the window. In all likelihood, the building was abandoned but if anyone did still remain, Patricia promised that this time, she would defend herself.

Craig Micklewright

2

2015

Gemma pulls up her knickers, a decidedly unsexy pair she'd procured from a thrift store, and her puss' (as she likes to call it) gives off a lingering sting. That fat oaf was a tad overzealous, she thinks, and his junk was rather girthy - not that she's an expert on size or length ... at least not yet.

Tellulah meanwhile is thumbing through a wad of bills and separating them into even halves, hopefully. Gemma suspects that 'Tellulah' isn't her actual name. *She seems your typical, freckled all-American girl, and not some refugee fresh off a boat.*

"See, told you it'd be worth the extra shift. Here's your share." the girl says, offering the money whilst kneeling on the bed, the sheets crumpled, various stains soaking through to the mattress and she's wearing nothing but bobbysocks.

Origin

Gemma pulls on a t-shirt, and approaches, taking her money and not bothering to count it. She doesn't entirely trust it'll all be there, but then again, the money has never really been the point. Glancing past her colleague in sex, she notices a clock on the wall - it's a few minutes past seven.

"Well, it's been fun an all, but… I really have to shoot now." She says, tugging on a pair of leggings then shoving her feet into her sketchers.

Tellulah climbs down off the bed, seemingly in no rush to dress. A layer of perspiration coats her skinny body. *It looks good in the red glow from the lamp*, Gemma observes.

"We could always continue this back at my place." She says suggestively and comes up close to Gemma.

Gemma smirks at the obvious come-on, "Nah doll face, I only eat out on the job."

An obviously disappointed Tellulah watches her walk away, exiting through a door, before flopping down on the bed again, suddenly wondering where her clothes had been flung.

"Hey, what's all this then?" Harry remarks as they roll up to a set of traffic lights on their way to Queens.

Blake observes a few crowds and demonstrations on the street, as well as art depicting the moon in various guises.

"Oh, it'll be the eclipse that's happening tonight. Guess this sort of event brings all the freaks and fanatics out."

"So, the guy lives above a bar around here, then? What's the plan?" Harry continues.

"Gemma says he was talking about going over to wherever they've supposedly got her brother. Could be a wild goose chase, but I dunno, I have a feeling this is the way to go. Him and Juanita are cooking something up. This whole eclipse situation ain't no coincidence neither."

"Your friend says he drives a VW van, with a picture of a fish on the side, so shouldn't be too hard to spot."

As the lights change, Harry's Volvo heads further into the district, the sidewalks lined with people, some dressed in costumes like it was mardi gras. Eventually they slow down and park up a few metres from a two-story building. The ground floor sports a large neon sign that says: 'The Watering Hole', with an image of a fisherman dangling a rod into a hole.

Harry sparks up a fat cigar as they observe the building from a distance. Blake glances to him as he creates smoke clouds in the car interior.

"Bringing back memories?" He asks, playing with a loose piece of gauze on his bandaged hand.

"Of stake outs? Yeah, you could say that." Harry replies.

"Do you remember that final night going after Thomas Winston?"

Harry breathes out some smoke, dabbing the ash through a gap in his window, "The Doll Maker? Sick animal. How could I forget?"

"Probably been ten years. What did he get? Four life sentences running consecutively?"

"What they could pin on him. He did far more than four, everyone knows it, we just couldn't make it stick."

Origin

Blake lowers his hand and looks across the street as memories come flooding back.

Years ago

Darren Maitland brought two steaming coffees back to a grey Volvo estate (looking almost new) as Harry sat at the wheel. It was winter and below zero centigrade out.

"How long has it been now?" Darren asked as he climbed in and passed a coffee to Harry.

He took the plastic cup from Darren, taking a sip through the slit in the cup's lid. It was just the right temperature.

Harry was sporting a slight beard and bushy moustache, his hair dark. He was wearing a padded over coat and fingerless gloves. Placing the coffee in a cup holder between the seats, he checked his watch. It had just turned 10:30 at night.

"Ten minutes. She should have called in by now." He answered.

Darren, hair a short brown crew cut beneath a woollen hat, shivered in the passenger seat, the winter air having never suited him, "It's not been long, maybe we should give her five more minutes."

Just then a BlackBerry phone buzzed on the dash, and Darren reached for it in an instant, "Chloe? Where are you?"

"Dormitory three, Omega Lambda House." came a woman's voice.

"Has he been in communication at all?" Darren continued.

"Yeah, just a moment ago. He wants to meet in the car park. I... I'm scared, sir."

Darren placed his coffee alongside Harry's before taking out a 9mm pistol from inside his jacket.

"Ok, get out of there, sweetheart, you've done swell. We're on our way."

Harry took that as his cue, unclipping his seatbelt and opening his door, climbing out as Darren did the same.

Heading into the grounds of the college, Harry and Darren were joined by several uniformed officers as they headed towards one of the sorority buildings. As Harry reached a set of double doors, a scream then pierced the night and he froze, taking out his own chunky revolver in reaction.

"What was that?" Darren remarked, looking up to a window where a light had come on, it's glow ominously bleeding onto the campus grounds. Slowly he stepped in front of Harry and tried the door, which clicked open. Gradually they entered as Harry signalled for the officers to head around the outskirts of the building.

Darren reached a second-floor corridor and met up with a hysterical Chloe, a young brown-haired girl wearing a duffel coat. He took her in his arms, consoling her.

"It's ok, I'm here." He reassured.

The girl was shaking in his hold, and gradually raised her head, tear-soaked eyes staring at him like she'd just experienced something terrible.

"Back there, room 12..." She said as her lips quivered.

Origin

Darren looked to Harry who cautiously ventured down the corridor where various other female students lingered, some in dressing gowns, others in pyjamas. He soon noticed the door to one room standing ajar.

"Ok, step aside ladies." Harry said, reaching the doorway and paused to push the door open fully, allowing the light within to illuminate the corridor, then walked inside.

Turning with a gasp, he laid eyes on two single beds, where presented on each was an image that would become engraved on his mind for years.

Two female students lay clothed in layered dresses as if from the eighteen hundreds, curly wigs on their heads, and their faces… as Harry approached, were wrapped in cling film, makeup painted on each to create a porcelain doll appearance. Harry lowered his gun, heart racing as he looked at the girls, their bodies horribly still, white tights on their legs and polished shoes on their feet. He looked at them as if they could be his own daughters… not that he'd had kids of his own, but regardless the anguish in his heart, felt like it could kill him.

"Get in here, Maitland!" He shouted as Darren appeared behind, instantly as horrified, Chloe lingering in the doorway, not daring to look again into the room.

"Fuck…" Darren exclaimed.

Harry raised a radio and spoke into it, "What you got, boys? Anything?"

Suddenly a gunshot rang out both through the radio's speaker and from outside. Darren looked to Harry, alarmed.

Craig Micklewright

Moments later, Darren burst out of the building's doors, jumping down the steps as he made for a nearby courtyard. The other officers had gathered in a small group, and Darren began to approach as Harry appeared at the doors behind him, slightly out of breath.

As Darren reached the group there was a moaning noise like someone was in pain. The officers let him through as he cast eyes on a middle aged, ordinary looking man on the ground, clutching a hand to his leg where he'd been shot.

The man glanced to Darren, quitting his moans of agony suddenly. Harry joined the group, shouting to the officers, with one checking a canvas bag, retrieving a stash of doll-like clothing.

"Ok, step aside boys, we got this. Nice work." - he then looked at the man, expecting some sort of monster, but was shocked at how pathetic he appeared.

"Cuff him. This sick freak is coming with us." Harry ordered.

As they both watched the man get pushed onto his front and his hands cuffed behind him, Darren's finger grew restless on the trigger of his pistol. *What would realistically happen if I just shot the son-of-a-bitch in the head?* He asked himself. Go to prison most likely, or everyone would turn a blind eye. Darren never found the courage to find out.

"Yeah, Thomas Winston killed four girls that night. He'd been there for over an hour before our contact even arrived. He had been playing us all along." Harry says as he continues

Origin

to observe the bar from within his Volvo, occasionally puffing on his cigar.

"So how many did we think he killed, in the end?" Blake asks.

"Easy double figures, but no way of coming up with an exact number. Winston's never said a word about it either, following the conviction. At least now he's rotting away his remaining years over on Rikers."

Just then a VW van pulls out of an alleyway beside the bar, an illustration of a fish on the side. Harry jolts in response.

"That's our guy. Ok let's do this." He remarks, starting up the engine and drives the Volvo out from behind a row of parked cars.

Blake looks to the road, eyes glued to the van as it proceeds two cars ahead. Praying with every fibre of his being, *this has to lead somewhere.*

3

Patricia explored the burnt-out interior of the sect's building, hoping for some kind of answer to aid her suspicions over Blake. She had seen him at his best and sadly, also his worst and understood how something like a person he cared about being attacked, might cause him to react in a way that wasn't the smartest. She recalled Lucas' threats, and feared her investigation might lead to a body. As much as she wasn't proud thinking it, she prayed it would be that of Mr Black, rather than her friend.

Stepping over singed debris, passing a charcoaled desk, she exited an office and proceeded down a corridor - her pistol in one hand, leading the way. Peeling posters still hung on walls advertising the sect like it was Scientology and not in fact a satanic cult. Images of that creature, of altars on biblical looking hill tops, gatherings of people with dark red sunsets, bleeding over the brainwashed.

Origin

She descended a staircase that creaked underfoot. The whole building felt like it could crumble any second. As she reached the bottom, she looked back up the stairs relieved, then started to feel slightly dizzy. Shaking the feeling off, she continued through another large office and headed towards the foyer where Blake and herself first met Lucas Black. It was becoming clear the place was abandoned and much of any clue to that man's whereabouts had likely been turned to ash. She felt hopeless as she approached the office they were previously ushered into, and as she reached for the doorknob - the dizzy feeling returned, this time, much stronger. Opening the door inwards, she staggered slightly. Grabbing at the door frame, she looked into a pitch-black interior then felt everywhere join it in total darkness. Her legs grew weak, the gun slipping from her grip, and she collapsed to the floor, passing out.

*

After what felt like only minutes but had actually been close to an hour, Patricia became aware of a voice calling her name. Initially the voice sounded like Blake. Wrinkling her nose up as she lay half inside the office, Patricia struggled to open her eyes, listening as the sound of her name changed, from a husky masculine voice to something younger... like a child.

"Patricia. Wake up... you must wake up!"

Her vision was blurry as she looked across the flooring to see two small feet in sneakers. Drool had formed a small puddle next to her mouth, and slowly, Patricia forced herself into a seating position, leaning against the door frame. Looking into the office, she was then amazed to find a little girl standing just a few feet away near a desk. She had blonde hair, wearing a blue tracksuit and immediately, Patricia knew who she was... but that was impossible.

"Jessica?" She said with disbelief.

"Hey there, Patricia. Good to see you. I was worried."

Patricia clambered against the door frame and stood up, feeling seriously out of sorts. Her head was throbbing.

"How is... how is this possible? You're..."

"Dead? Yes, but lucky for you, I'm here to show you something. But you must hurry, before it's too late."

Jessica walked around the burnt shell of the desk where Patricia and Blake had their meeting with the, at the time, charming Lucas Black.

The young girl then picked out a sheet of paper from a filing tray, tossing it onto the desk as Patricia reached the other side.

Lying before her was what looked to be a tax bill, the edges of the paper singed. *Huh, runs a satanic cult but still stays in good with the IRS? Go figure*, Patricia mused as she picked up the letter, casting her eyes over it.

"What am I supposed to do with this?" She asked young Jessica.

"Hazard a guess that'll be Mr Black's home address. If your friend was looking for him, he might have gone there. So, get a move on now."

Patricia focused on the little girl, her heart crying out at seeing her again. She had so wanted to help her, having played what happened over in her head, to answer questions she

Origin

didn't want the answer to, like… had she caused this innocent girl's death by trying to force answers out of her relating to those that kidnapped her?

"Now, you be careful Patricia, don't push yourself too hard, not in your condition." Jessica continued as Patricia folded the letter up and placed it in her handbag.

"I know, I just got out of hospital, the operation…"

"Not that, silly… the baby."

Patricia stared at the girl in shock, "How'd you…"

Jessica walked around the desk to Patricia. At just over three feet, she was tiny next to her.

"Listen, you've not just got yourself to think of now. So be careful. Find Blake and walk away, from all of this."

Jessica's large elfin eyes had a wisdom to them beyond her years. Patricia hadn't noticed it until now.

"This is crazy. Why am I seeing you, here, now Jessica?"

"Maybe I never left your subconscious, after… you know."

Patricia smiled and reached down to touch the little girl's shoulder, squeezing it affectionately.

"I'm so sorry, Jessica. I could never have imagined that happening to you. Can you ever forgive me?"

"You have nothing to be forgiven for. A higher order took me, and if you're not careful … it will come for you, Blake and anyone you care about. Please, stop Blake and walk away."

As Patricia listened, she took the letter back out of her bag, unfolding it to read the address again, "Yes I know you're right, thank you Jess…" then looking again, she discovered she was alone in the office. The little girl had vanished.

After a while, Patricia sat in the back of a cab, neon lights from the street flashing the window, the road ahead full of traffic.

"Crazy what happened back there, huh?" The Mexican driver remarked.

Patricia, lost in her own thoughts, looked to the front cabin, "Sorry, what was that?"

"Where I picked you up. That building was torched the other night. Big blaze. I tell ya, it was an insurance job."

"Oh right, I… I was just passing by. Did anyone see anything?"

"Apparently not, señora, whoever did it was real careful."

Patricia watched the city wiz by the window, unsure of where things were leading but as Jessica had said, she had to stop Blake before events spiralled out of control, if they hadn't already.

The cab arrived in a classy suburban neighbourhood shortly after, and Patricia shouted out as she spotted something. The driver slammed on the breaks, the cab screeching to a halt. Patricia climbed out, hurrying to pay and thank the driver before rushing across the street. Parked in a side alley between two buildings was to her dismay, the unmistakable sight of Blake's Honda HR-V.

"Oh Blake, you dumb idiot." She cursed out loud before turning and continuing on, illuminated by overhead street lamps.

Origin

Soon she came before a large gate in the centre of tall stone walls. She checked the address with a quick look at the letter, before staring apprehensively to a house some distance beyond. Approaching the medieval-looking iron gate, Patricia pushed against it to discover a large chain hanging loose, like someone had applied bolt cutters. Easing the gate open a little way, she quickly headed up a driveway, overhanging palm trees framing it as the large building loomed ominously ahead.

Reaching a door, she paused realising that entering through the main entrance might not be the cleverest move, and quickly headed around the house, glancing to a large front window on the way - the house interior appearing lifeless. *Was this just going to be a dead end?* Either way she was here now.

Taking out her gun she proceeded down a path beside the house, making her way to the rear. She soon entered a rear patio area. There was a large swimming pool and a barbecue area. *How, er... ordinary,* she observed - although what was she expecting, Dracula in his castle? She reached a door with a shutter on it, which she opened to reveal a broken window, and her sneaker-clad feet crunched fragments of glass. She quickly realised she may be retreading Blake's footsteps, and felt her nerves getting the better of her as she opened the door and ventured inside.

Walking into a spacious kitchen, Patricia found a glass of red wine on a counter in the kitchen, and on the floor lay a shattered bottle. The scene told its own story. Patricia followed wine-stained footprints out into a hallway where they led, gradually fading, towards a door. Patricia then became aware of the sound of an engine running and approached, hesitantly trying the handle. The door creaked as it opened, leading into a garage that had a strong stench of gasoline. She proceeded down a couple of stone steps to see a large SUV parked, its engine rumbling. As she approached pointing her gun, she found a hose attached to the tail pipe.

That horrible feeling that hadn't left her from the moment Detective Davenport told her Blake hadn't been seen, cranked itself up to eleven as she walked around to the front of the vehicle. Lowering the gun in her hand, she held her other hand to her mouth on discovering Lucas Black sitting, motionless in the front. His head was slumped to one side, as if sleeping - but Patricia knew he wasn't. The man was dead. Spotting the other end of the hose poking in through a rear window, she then tried the door, but it was locked. Stepping back, she then collided with a set of shelves, causing some garden tools to fall and clatter noisily. Suddenly scared, she pocketed her gun and rushed away.

On re-entering the house, she was met by a figure several feet ahead, partially illuminated by a shard of moonlight beaming in from the kitchen.

"Blake." She announced in recognition.

He walked forward, looking puzzled, "Patricia, how the hell…"

"What have you done, Blake? Jesus Christ. Are you insane?"

Blake raised both hands as if gesturing to her could defuse the situation, "Now, listen… I didn't plan any of this… Black, he… he hurt you really bad."

Origin

"But I'm here Blake, I'm alive… and he's… fuck, was you going for a suicide set up? For Christ's sake."

"I was just making sure I'd covered my tracks when I heard a noise come from the garage…. Like he was still…"

"Breathing? No, I've just seen him. He looked dead as dead to me. Have you any idea what this has done, you going rogue like this? The case is now as dead as… as…. as that little girl!!"

Patricia then clutched a hand to her temple and felt her brain rattle in her skull. It was suddenly like a thousand voices all shouting at once.

"Hey, what is it?" Blake remarked, reaching her and touched a hand to her upper arm area.

Patricia looked at him, eyes widening as she felt a jolt of pain hit her. She fell against the wall, crying out as Blake panicked, and she collapsed to the floor, suddenly going into a seizure.

Blake stood over her, at a loss of what to do, watching as Patricia began to shake violently.

"Patricia!!" He yelped, then looked around himself before rushing back down the hallway.

Blake's Honda backed up to the front of the house. He applied the handbrake and climbed out, heading to the rear of the building. Minutes later, he was carrying Patricia in his arms down the side pathway, looking around himself nervously as he returned to his car. She was semi-conscious and murmuring deliriously, whilst tears streamed down Blake's face. This was the worst imagined outcome. He had gone after Lucas Black because of Patricia. He had not expected his actions to further risk her health.

Eventually he climbed into the driver's side, where Patricia was slumped within her seatbelt next to him.

"Stay strong there, hun, I'll get you fixed, I promise." He said out loud, then adjusted the gear stick and trod down on the gas.

Origin

4

Springdale

Gemma approaches her bike, unlocking a chain that was securing it to a lamp post outside the brothel building. Taking a water bottle from under the seat, she unfastens the cap and relieves her thirst, before screwing the cap back on - then as she goes to slot the bottle back in place, suddenly she jolts and stiffens. A sharp, electrical shock hits the bottom of her spine. She collapses to the ground as behind her, a pocket taser sparking in one hand, stands Juanita.

"You and I gonna have a little chat, girlie." She remarks as a dazed Gemma lies twitching and unable to move at her feet.

A short while later, Gemma comes round, finding herself lying on a couch in Juanita's office. Feeling dizzy, she looks over to Juanita who is seated behind her desk at a computer.

"Hey, what gives?" Gemma groans.

"Gemma Saint, nice name… not that girls who come work for me ever give their true identity. Goes with the territory. So, what's your story, kid?"

Gemma sits up, dropping her feet to the floor, then recalls the electrical shock she was dealt. A cold feeling wraps around her body like being hugged by a snowman.

Juanita gets up, walking around to the front of her desk, and rests against it as Gemma spots a gun tucked into the front of her embroidered jeans.

"Decided to close up shop early - Momma's got a few things on tonight. I was looking through the CCTV, which I'm guessing you wasn't aware of. My cameras are hidden you see. A woman in my position can never be too careful. Well, who do I recognise hangin' around by my door only a few hours ago? None other than your white-trash self. Were you listening in on my meeting with Drago, Gemma? If that's even your name."

Gemma struggles to find an explanation that would come across as legit. So she goes for the first thing she can think of.

"I never liked that guy, Juanita. He scares me… I guess I was just… looking out for you."

"An honourable thing to say, but then I checked my other cameras, outside and… what I overheard has rather disturbed me."

Origin

Gemma looks to the office door, wondering if it's locked. She notices a key inserted in the doorknob, and asks herself: *can I reach it before this Spanish bitch pulls that piece she's packing?*

Juanita turns the computer's screen 180 degrees and hits a key on the keyboard, playing a piece of recorded footage. Gemma's heartbeat intensifies as she sees herself in the alley, speaking on her cell.

'Hey guys. I can't stay on long. I got some news. You're gonna want to get on this straight away I think.'

Juanita presses a key on the keyboard again, pumping up the volume until the noise of passing traffic can be heard. Gemma grows increasingly nervous, seeing herself, hood up but recognisable.

'I managed to hear some stuff. This big fuckin' dude called 'Drago', he's going some place later. They're holding someone, a hostage I think, and it's all to do with the eclipse that's happening tonight. They said they brought him over from Chicago. That's where I'm from, and where Kai went missing. Listen to me when I say, this ain't no fuckin' coincidence.'

With that, Juanita pauses the recording and takes what Gemma recognises as a small wallet from the desk - her clutch purse. She then removes an I.D. card.

"Gemma Mathews. From Chicago. Cabrini Green to be precise. Hmm, tough neighbourhood. So, your brother's Kai Mathews, huh? He's also a friend of some of my associates over there. Kai has been so generous, volunteering himself for tonight's proceedings."

Gemma suddenly gets up, just as Juanita pulls the gun on her lightning-fast. Gemma freezes.

Craig Micklewright

"Where you holding him?"

"I'd admire you if I didn't also think you were fucking stupid. Who were you speaking to on the phone? Who else is involved in this master plan of yours? They didn't have a blonde mullet by any chance?"

"I wasn't talking to nobody you'd know." Gemma retorts, any bravado and hope slipping out of her like water through a cheese grater.

She feels herself start to panic. How on earth is she meant to get out of this one? Juanita places the purse to one side then holds up Gemma's cell.

"Unlock it." She says, holding the phone out whilst keeping the gun pointed with her other hand.

Hesitantly, Gemma approaches, her nerves playing hell. She reaches out for the phone, then suddenly grabs a tape dispenser and slams it against Juanita's head, causing her to fall backwards over the desk, the gun going off and blasting a hole in the ceiling. Gemma darts to the door, grabbing the handle, and twists the key in the lock; the door opens.

Juanita clambers against the desk, grabbing her gun and fires three more times as she sees Gemma flee, bullets hitting the door and splintering part of the doorframe. She staggers after her, stumbling into the corridor but sees Gemma disappear around the corner. As she goes to aim the gun, Juanita then spots smatterings of blood on the floor. Taking a breath, a grin slowly forms on her face.

*

Origin

Drago opens a set of gates to a large storage complex, where several buildings tower a number of floors above. With evening drawing in, clouds and a darkening sky loom overhead. He checks a pricey-looking rotary watch on his wrist and sees that it's just gone 7:30 p.m.

He then hears a melody and pauses from entering the complex to retrieve his phone from his jacket.

"Juanita? Hey, wait up. Calm down. What is it?"

Juanita gets into her silver Mercedes outside the brothel and starts up the engine. She's nursing a bloody gash to her brow with a tissue, more blood running down her face to stain the collar of her blouse.

"There's been a fuckin' development! You need to be on your guard. I'm on my way to you now but… we're not alone in this anymore."

"What's gone on?" Drago asks, as he climbs back into his van and drives it into the grounds, the headlights illuminating a large shutter to the main building. He pauses in the front cabin as Juanita responds.

Driving out of an alleyway and onto the main road, she treads down on the gas as she talks, "We had a situation going on right under our noses. A spy you might call it. You know that girl from a month back, Gemma?"

Drago shuts off the van's engine and climbs out, walking to the shutter and unlocking it. He then tugs at a chain, causing the shutter to slowly rise.

234

"That kid who golden showered all over my face? Huh, yeah, I like her."

"You won't for much longer." Juanita's voice says, "Firstly, I'm gonna fuckin' kill her, if she ain't dead already."

Drago looks surprised, "Why? What happened, Juanita?"

"I had her, that deceitful *puta*. After I took her in and gave her a job. How does she repay me? By all this time lying to my face! Turns out, she's our friend's little sister. She's Kai's sister. I… I don't know what she was up to but she's not working alone. I dunno, Drago, I'm thinking that we pull the plug on this whole deal."

Drago peers into a large warehouse, some light flickering within, "Listen, Juanita. Regardless of what has or hasn't occurred … are you suddenly forgetting about Carlos? What happened?! This has been professed, you know that. Since the dark times. Our lord Nefalym will show us the way, bring the world into the darkness it deserves and make us disciples. Carlos gave his life to a greater calling. We owe it to his memory to finish what he was unknowingly a part of."

Juanita heads into the city, occasionally checking her reflection in the rear-view mirror. The cut looks like it's going to need stitches.

"I know, Drago. I think about Carlo every day and what he sacrificed."

Drago walks into the warehouse, and the shutter falls down loudly behind him.

"We can't change our plans. We've come too far. Lest we forget everything that has led to this night: the setbacks we've

Origin

endured from the less enlightened, like that coward 'Lucas Black' offing himself last year, or the 'sisters' taking matters into their own hands and causing the Miami incident. Tonight… will not fail, *we* cannot fail."

At that same time, around the corner from the entrance to the factory complex, sits Harry's Volvo.

"What are we waiting for then?" Harry asks impatiently.

Blake checks his watch, looking lost in his own thoughts.

"Blake?" Harry adds, and Blake looks to him.

"This whole deal, whatever they're planning, is likely happening when the eclipse occurs. We go rushing in now, we'll never know what they're trying to achieve. We need to catch them in the act… it's the only way to…"

"Only way to what?"

"Find out exactly what's been happening, Harry - for years now, firstly in New York, then Miami, what's begun but never finished. We need to see this for ourselves."

"You're not making sense."

"No, Harry… the scary thing is, I'm actually making perfect sense."

Harry just stares at Blake as an unnerving sensation develops in the pit of his stomach.

Craig Micklewright

5

Drago walks down a corridor within the warehouse and reaches a door. Producing a set of keys from within his long trench coat, he unlocks the door, and with a squeak of rusted hinges, allows himself entry. The room he walks into is large with minimal furnishing. In the centre is a young blonde-haired man, positioned on his knees before what appears to be an altar, going by the flickering candles and a carved statue of the goat-like demon. He's consumed in prayer.

"Kai..." Drago says, causing the man, who seems initially unaware of Drago's arrival, to jolt.

He opens his eyes as his whispered words pause, then looks to the tall Spaniard.

"Juanita has just rang. She says there's been an incident. An outside party, or parties appear to be trying to intervene."

Origin

"What outside parties?" the man responds - he's skinny, bare-chested wearing nothing more than sweatpants; feet bare, cuts and grazes disfiguring his arms and chest.

"It's under control. Nobody will interfere with what we have planned, I assure you. You seem… calmer today."

"Our lord has shown me guidance. Tells me I shouldn't be impatient. We will be as one soon enough."

Drago looks around the room. It's dusty but otherwise clean, "That's reassuring. Juanita will be here soon. The moon is already high in the sky. Are you sure you're ready?"

Kai lowers his head, bowing before the altar, "I have been ready for weeks." He replies, as his thoughts drift back to the day he first decided to give his life over to a demonic deity.

Chicago,
December

Kai Matthews sat in the passenger seat of an old beaten-up Fiesta as a young, Italian-looking woman was at the wheel, parking the vehicle outside a single floor building. Shutting off the rattling engine, she looked to Kai inquisitively. Thick eyeliner and a septum piercing in her nose created a stereotypical punk-goth image, complete with customised clothing and black painted fingernails. In comparison Kai wasn't quite as made up, other than his lengthy blonde hair being greased back, wearing an over coat, a black Rammstein t-shirt and skinny jeans.

"You're quiet. What's up, Kai?" She asked inquisitively.

"Nothing. I'm fine." came Kai's abrupt response.

238

He climbed out of the car, slamming the door which threatened to cause the whole vehicle to collapse, and the girl watched him approach the building. With a sigh she removed her seatbelt and followed.

The building was a clubhouse, a large room with a bar at one end with various seating areas dotted around. The lighting was minimal with a small stage located to the far right, and cigarette smoke hung in the air like a giant cobweb. Kai met up with a group of similarly dressed members, many sporting tattoos, dyed hair and numerous piercings. To an outsider it likely resembled some kind of convention. The Italian girl, who had been calling herself 'Widow' for a year or two, was greeted by another girl and they swapped air kisses, all the time Widow not taking her eyes off Kai. He hadn't been acting right for days, had been consumed in his own world. Deep down she knew it was all related to the organisation they were a part of. She had brought him onboard a couple of years back following drunken sex in a nightclub toilet. To her it was family, a place where she could belong. To Kai however, it had become much more, and it was starting to concern her.

"Kai!" someone then shouted, and Widow looked from him to a tall figure standing near the bar. He was dark skinned.

Kai parted from the group and made his way over to the tall man, and they hugged.

"I'm so glad you're here. Can you spare a minute to join me in the back office?" The man asked.

Origin

Kai looked to the man and nodded as Widow watched from a distance, seeing him get escorted behind the bar and out of her viewpoint.

Kai seated himself before a desk in a small office and glanced around to the various posters on the walls, depicting rock bands like Black Sabbath and Slipknot. The tall man he knew as Drago, one of the founders of The Sect of the Fallen Angel. It made his pulse race that he was here, and watched as he sat himself down the other side.

"A few of my closest confidants have informed me of your development. I thought I'd attend tonight to have this little chat with you, hope that's ok." Drago said.

"Of course, sir." Kai responded.

"You see in a few weeks there's going to be an occasion we'd like you to be a part of."

"Ok…"

"The high priestess will be there."

"Juanita?"

Drago smiled, "Yes, her base of operations, New York has been chosen as the location for a very important ceremony. We are planning on making contact you see, and this time we'll be requiring a host. A body for our Lord to inhabit, temporarily of course."

"Oh."

"It's been a long time coming. The forthcoming Lunar Eclipse has been foretold as the night in question. It could be years before our little following gets another chance such as this."

240

Kai fidgeted uncomfortably in his seat, not making eye contact, "So what is my part?"

"I'm glad you ask. We were hoping that your faith was pure enough to take on the role of Lord Nefalym's vessel."

Kai looked at Drago. He had imagined stepping up, being more significant, but this?

"That would... be an honour, sir." He said.

Drago offered a wide grin then got up, walking around the table as Kai joined him, and he wrapped an arm around his shoulders, squeezing tight.

"That's my boy! Few people in history ever get an opportunity like this. You will be remembered, I assure you."

A knock came to the office door and they both looked over.

"Come in." Drago shouted.

The door opened and a man peered in looking concerned.

"Sorry to bother you, sir... there's a woman outside asking to see her brother. She got quite aggressive when we told her it was members only."

Kai suddenly felt nervous.

"Did she say who it was she was looking for?"

"It was Mr Matthews, sir..." the man said offering a look to Kai.

Drago returned to the main room as Kai followed. From behind the bar, he could see over to the glass entrance doors and the men who had been posted outside, where a hooded figure was also visible.

"You best go talk to her, but she doesn't come inside, you understand?" Drago said to Kai who nodded then hurried around the bar.

Origin

Widow watched as Kai headed for the entrance as she stood sipping from a plastic cup of coke, having been chatting with a few of the others. She was all too aware of who it was and realised this could mean trouble.

Kai pushed through the two well-built men who had been placed at the entrance, to be met by a short, young woman dressed in a hoodie and leggings: his kid sister, Gemma.

"What the fuck, Kai?!" She exclaimed, eyes a mixture of anger and concern.

Kai grabbed her by one arm and marched her away, "What are you doing here, Gem'?"

"What am I doing here? It's been weeks. You haven't been home. What's got into you, bro?"

"Nothing's got into me. This is who I am, Gem'. You, Mom, Dad have to understand that. This is my life now."

"What, with these Marilyn Manson dropouts? Fuckin' hell Kai, get your head straight. They're a bunch of fuckin' weirdos!"

"No they're not! Beats getting drunk every night and screwin' around like you most of the time."

Gemma looked incensed and stepped forward shoving her hand to his chest.

"I'm not a whore you motherfucker!"

Kai stumbled back before retaliating and thrusting both hands to her shoulders, causing Gemma to stagger and fall over.

She landed in a muddy puddle as her hood fell back, exposing untidy blonde hair. She sat looking upset.

"Oh, Gemma… sorry, hey let me help you up." He said with a smirk and offered his hand.

Gemma looked up and splashed some dirty water back at him to soak his trousers. Kai stared at her sternly then stormed away. Gemma was left feeling humiliated as Kai headed back to the clubhouse, not looking back.

*

Kai raises his head again, mumbling under his breath as Drago stands beside him in the warehouse.

"Everyone will be here soon. I'll come back when we're ready to begin." Drago says then walks away, echoing footsteps gradually fading.

Briefly Kai pictures his sister, looking pathetic sitting in that muddy puddle - the last time that he saw her.

"You'll understand, one day Gem'." He whispers.

In an alleyway somewhere, Gemma walks drunkenly, tripping against boxes and discarded litter whilst brushing against a wall of a building. A smear of blood is left on the brickwork and her breath has become laboured. She stops, a stabbing pain just below her ribs and checks her hand that's covered in blood. Lifting the hem of her top she finds an open wound where one of Juanita's gunshots must have caught her.

"Shit." She remarks, more for the inconvenience than any serious concern, then proceeds awkwardly on, every step a growing struggle.

Origin

6

(8:15p.m.)

A series of vehicles pass by Harry's Volvo, their tires kicking up dirt and gravel. Once they've gone, both Blake and Harry sit upright having been ducking out of view. Harry looks to Blake and opens his door.

"It's show time." He remarks and claims out.

Blake feels adrenaline kick in and follows suit, soon meeting Harry on the sidewalk. Approaching chain-link fencing they can see into the vast complex where various vehicles arrive outside one of the buildings.

"Maybe we need to call backup?"

Blake walks on, "We'll take that step only if necessary, come on... let's get closer."

Harry looks up to the sky and suddenly notices an ominous sight... the full moon above has a large curved shadow partially cast over it. *This is it,* he thinks. He then notices a growing crowd of people congregate around the building, just as a large shutter opens, revealing a tanned man in a trench coat.

"Welcome loyal subjects!" Drago bellows, holding both arms out, then steps aside to let everyone into the warehouse.

Mingled voices pass through the group, a mixture of excitement and trepidation in the air. Near the back stands Widow. Her dark eyes jumping from face to face, most of them strangers to her. In all truth, she has shy'd away from the Sect since Kai left Chicago. She's not entirely certain why she's even here, but regardless, she needs to see her boyfriend again.

Ten minutes earlier

Gemma staggered out onto the street as she watched several vehicles pass by. Clutching a hand to her side, she winced in agony, lost for answers as to where she was going or what she was doing. In all likelihood, she could be in serious trouble with how her wound was bleeding... shouldn't she be in the emergency room?

Before she could contemplate further, a beaten-up Fiesta paused at the traffic lights. Steadying herself by a street sign, she looked to the driver then noticed a goth styled girl. *Widow,* her brother's girlfriend. *Fuck, if she's in New York, then...*

As the Fiesta drove on, Gemma went to call out but thought better of it, darting across the road as she saw the car turn down another street. Rushing onwards, avoiding traffic,

Origin

she attempted to follow, all the time keeping the car in view, despite it getting further and further away.

After a moment, she reached a street corner, wheezing and coughing. God dammit, she was in pain! Looking to her sneakers, she noticed spots of blood stain her left foot, along with more spots hitting the sidewalk. Her breath was struggling now. She hated to think it but… *was time running out?* It was like she was an hourglass and her gradually depleting blood was the sand.

She then noticed the Fiesta zoom across the road up ahead, coughing out black smoke. As it turned onto another street, a large sign stood pointing, stencilled words saying 'Townsend Shipping & Storage'. With an intake of breath, Gemma hurried across the street, desperate for her wild goose chase to finally bear fruit.

*

Blake slowly creeps beside one parked van, peeking his head out in time to observe the twenty plus strong group enter the warehouse. The shutter comes crashing down behind them and he looks around to check he's alone. With a gun gripped in one hand, he reaches the rear doors of the van and finds one door to be open. Grabbing the handles, he pulls both doors open, peering in to see several cardboard boxes, lids removed, with what appears to be clothing within, as well as masks. Taking a mask in hand, he once again checks around himself, before turning it over to see that it resembles the goat-like demon. He places the mask aside, reaching into the box again, retrieving a black robe. Suddenly he jolts as Harry comes behind him.

"Jesus, Harry… don't do that!" Blake gasps before showing his friend and former mentor the boxes, "Check this shit out. Looks like we got a way in."

Harry picks up one of the masks with fascination.

"You realise this could be suicide, Blake." He responds.

Blake looks at him, "If you were so worried about that, old man, you wouldn't be here. Time to play dress up!"

Minutes later the congregation are gathered in the large room within the warehouse, gradually forming a wide circle and are all wearing the long black hooded robes and goat masks. Drago approaches Kai who stands before the altar, and they turn around. A few mingled voices radiate from the group until Drago raises his hand. He also wears a gown, although his is dark red in colour and he's not wearing a mask.

"Friends, followers… Let me begin by thanking you all for being here tonight. Scripture has spoken of this exact night for centuries and we should all feel a great honour that we are here now, to witness this moment in history."

A few claps and cheers are briefly heard. Towards the back of one section of the gathered circle, stand two figures in identical robes and masks. The one looks to the other as if reacting to Drago's words.

"Without further hesitation, may I request that the sky light is opened?" Drago continues, as another robed figure over by a pulley mechanism starts to tug at a series of cords.

High above on the warehouse's ceiling a sky light shutter is gradually opened, bathing the room with a feint red beam

Origin

of light. As the shutter opens fully, a groan of wonder rings out from everyone, to see that the skylight is shaped like a crucifix. The glow however, creates an upside-down red cross of light directly over the altar and where Kai stands.

A few mingled voices circulate amongst the group, the noise building as just then from the far right, a figure in a long silver coloured robe appears and approaches the centre of the room.

Reaching Kai, the figure removes its hood to reveal themself as Juanita Equarez - The High Priestess. She has a small bandaid above her right eye, clearly the best she could manage to hide her injury.

Silence is restored as everyone anticipates her words. Juanita momentarily touches Kai's bare chest with her hand and long painted fingernails, then turns to face her congregation.

"The blood moon is upon us! We have waited long for this. Tonight, we will change the course of history." She says to approving ears.

From within her robe, she then reveals the dagger. Near the back of the circle of people, one figure goes to react until another touches their arm, shaking their head.

Juanita turns to Kai and offers him the dagger, "Open yourself for our lord Nefalym, create the gateway." She says.

Kai looks to the golden dagger, its large curved blade glinting in a mist of red moonlight. He takes it from Juanita and applies the blade to his hand. Turning back to the altar, with a wince of pain he pulls the blade over his open palm and a crimson gush drips over the effigy of the demon.

Of the two figures at the back, one takes out a revolver, keeping it low and out of sight. A cry of terror then echoes through the room, and immediately one of the figures pushes forward, quickly followed by the other. Shoving their way through the group, they then discover Juanita struggling - a young girl has grabbed her from behind.

Kai looks to her shocked, "Gemma?!?"

Gemma has Juanita in a choke hold, a broken shard of glass to her face. Drago approaches and reveals a gun of his own.

"Let her go! Nobody has to die here!" Drago shouts.

Suddenly Harry steps out from the group as he shrugs his hood off and removes the mask, pointing his revolver towards Drago, Juanita and Gemma.

"Police! Everyone calm down. Backup is on the way, drop your weapons!"

Drago goes to turn and aim his gun just as a shot rings out and he's blasted off his feet to fall to the floor, clutching his arm as his gun slides out of reach.

Blake removes his mask as he aims his own gun, smoke filtering into the air from the nozzle. Harry glances to him then refocuses on Juanita.

Kai still stands by the altar and has barely reacted. Gemma looks over to him as tears roll down her cheeks. She's desperately holding onto Juanita whilst struggling herself to remain standing. The hand holding the glass shard is shaking for all to see. The gathered members of the congregation slowly back away.

Origin

From the group another figure then emerges dressed in grungy clothing consisting of a patchwork shirt, torn jeans and leather boots.

"Time to come home, Kai." Widow says gently and Kai turns his head, revealing, much to everyone's shock, glowing yellow eyes.

Each member of the congregation lets out a gasp. Suddenly Juanita elbows Gemma right in her wound, who cries out before stumbling and dropping to the floor. Lying slightly supported on her elbows, she watches Juanita approach Kai. Harry backs off in horror, switching the aim of his gun over to the yellow-eyed man.

"Lose the knife, son." He remarks.

Kai looks to him, then before Juanita can reach him, he thrusts a hand back and she's sent flying into the air, crashing to the floor seconds after. Cries erupt as panic ensues; members suddenly running for their lives as Kai grabs Harry's wrist. The revolver discharges but the bullet bounces inexplicably off Kai's face. Blake runs forward, shoving him into the altar, causing it to topple as everything crashes to the floor, lit candles rolling away to hit a far wall where ceremonial banners hang, which instantly catch fire.

Harry looks to Blake in alarm just as Widow runs to where Gemma lies. She helps her to stand and notices a thick patch of blood soaking through her top.

"You alright, girl?"

"Get the fuck off of me!" Gemma shouts and pulls away from Widow.

250

As the others make their escape, hurrying to the outer corridor, as well as fleeing through a side entrance … Gemma approaches where Kai now lies. He's whimpering and there's a pool of blood spreading out beneath. Her eyes widen in distress as she crouches and touches his shoulder.

"Hey, watch out young lady!" Harry remarks, gun poised at the ready.

Blake lingers in the background beside Widow.

"It's… it's ok, he's… he's my b- brother." Gemma says, barely able to form words as blood drips on the floor.

Harry notices and goes to her aid, just as Kai rolls over, revealing the dagger imbedded in his chest.

Blake places a hand over his own mouth, realising he may have caused such a turn of events.

"Kai!" Gemma exclaims and collapses beside him, draping her arm around his neck as he turns his head to look at her.

"Gem'?" He groans, blood escaping his mouth as he speaks.

Blake looks around. To his far left, Juanita remains motionless in a heap on the floor. He then looks to Drago who is nursing his blasted shoulder. Neither appear to pose any further threat. He lowers his gun and comes to Harry's side.

"We should call an ambulance." He says, then Harry points to Gemma and Kai.

"Might be too late for this one." He replies as Blake looks to Kai, his eyes lifeless as Gemma holds onto him, sobbing her heart out.

Widow joins them, looking distraught.

Origin

"Oh no…" She comments with obvious remorse.

Harry looks to the rising flames as the fire that began by the banners travels to neighbouring cardboard boxes, crates and the wooden walls of the warehouse, quickly escalating.

"We need to go. Now!" He announces, then reaches for Gemma, tucking his gun away as he pulls her off of Kai.

"Noooo!" She cries.

"He's gone, Gemma. Come on, kid or we'll all be next!"

Widow backs off reluctantly, then turns and makes for the nearest exit as Harry follows, cradling Gemma in his arms. Blake remains to observe the scene, and watches Drago stagger over to Juanita, pulling her up in his arms and lifting her unconscious body. Blake decides to not intervene and starts to walk away also, the glow of the fire quickly joined by clouds of smoke.

Outside, Harry lies a pale and incredibly weak Gemma on the ground as Widow joins him. Drago carries Juanita out then collapses to his knees, overcome by smoke inhalation as he coughs and splutters. Harry then tosses his cell phone to Widow who catches it, and he takes out a set of old handcuffs, walking over to Drago.

"Call 911! Get an ambulance here or that girl's gonna die!" He shouts to Widow who complies, opening the phone and tapping numbers.

Harry thrusts Drago onto his front and applies the cuffs. The guy seems beyond struggling, his attempts feeble beneath Harry's weight.

Back in the burning warehouse interior, Blake heads towards the corridor just as he hears something; a sound like the earth is cracking open. Looking back, he can just make out the red glow of the lunar eclipse as it bleeds into the building from the skylight. Clouds of smoke distort his vision but he's able to see where a large hole has appeared, matching the shape of the reverse crucifix. Walking back to it he stares in disbelief at steps leading down into the dark. Glancing around, the room is otherwise devoid of life… Kai's dead body slumped against the remnants of the altar. Blake walks around the cross-shaped hole and reaches Kai. He then takes the dagger from his chest.

Outside, Harry stands looking down at Gemma, "How long they say they'd be?"

Widow comes to his side, the phone in one hand, "Didn't say, but… I told them to hurry. How she doing?"

"I really don't know. She's holding on, but just barely." Harry says with dismay.

"Where's your friend?" Widow then enquires.

As if suddenly reminded of Blake, Harry turns and rushes back to the warehouse entrance.

"Blake?!" He shouts, waving his hands against the billowing smoke - then holds his arm to his nose and mouth, before venturing inside.

In the warehouse, the place has become engulfed in flames. Harry re-enters the large room and rushes towards the centre, then halts as he discovers the hole. Looking around, there is no sign of Blake. Then as he refocuses on the hole, it collapses in on itself, leaving nothing but a small crater.

Origin

Unable to linger any longer, he backs off then reluctantly makes for the exit again.

Coughing repeatedly, he returns to see Widow knelt at Gemma's side, pressing a hand firmly to the girl's waist in an attempt to stop the bleeding. Harry stands confused, overwhelmed, not knowing what to think or say. As he looks to the sky, a full, blood-red moon looming, he prays that Blake made it out.

Craig Micklewright

7

The darkness is all consuming. Blake can barely see his hand in front of his face, only aware of his echoing footsteps on what feels like hard stone flooring. He can't even be sure how long he's been walking since reaching the bottom of the steps, his senses becoming mixed up and confused. Making the choice to venture into the hole, albeit away from the danger of a burning building, quickly begins to feel like a mistake.

As he proceeds, a slight clinical smell drifts under his nose. Reaching out he feels a wall to his side and runs his hand along it in the dark, until he reaches a doorknob. Stopping in his tracks he curls his fingers around then turns it. Something clicks and he pushes, immediately flooding bright light into wherever he is standing. The light blinds him momentarily making him close his eyes, until he finds the courage to open them again and discovers he's in a hospital room.

Origin

"Patricia?" He says with astonishment as a doctor stands by a bed holding a clipboard, and a nurse straightens a pillow.

"How's she doing, Doctor?" the young nurse enquires.

The doctor observes Patricia lying unconscious, then checks his clipboard, "She came through the operation well, we managed to stop the bleed on the brain."

They both look at her with interest, just as Blake, now back in his usual attire, comes to the end of the bed, recognising his friend. Damn, he had almost forgot how bad she had been... and knew it was all his fault.

"I'm doing ok now, Blake." a voice then echoes, and Blake looks back to the door to see Patricia standing there, cradling her newborn baby in her arms. This version of her however, is blossoming, beautiful, hair styled in a pixie cut, wearing a flowing summer dress. Blake turns around and walks up to her. His nostrils flair at discovering how good she also smells.

"Patricia, I..." – words fail him.

Patricia glares at him, "You almost killed me. You came so close..."

"No, I didn't... I was just..."

The baby girl in Patricia's arms gurgles slightly, catching Blake's attention.

"It's ok, I understand." Patricia continues, "But now that I have Jessica... you really can't be in my life anymore. You're poison, Blake, you always have been."

Blake looks at her face again, "Patricia. You don't mean that."

Patricia then smiles, a wicked glint to her eyes, leaning closer as she replies, "Oh yes I do."

Craig Micklewright

Suddenly everything goes pitch black. Blake stumbles forward as if attempting to touch Patricia but she's no longer there. Walking blindly, he feels the ground grow softer, and his shoes crunch on something brittle and slushy. Squinting his eyes, he starts to make out something, a light... in the distance. As he grows closer, the light grows brighter. *Is this what it feels like,* he ponders, *to be walking to the other side, to one's death?*

He then begins to make out the light, realising that it's coming from a house, a single light emanating from a front door. As he reaches a snow-covered street, he recognises his old house, from over in Brooklyn. Looking around himself, the other houses are blanketed in darkness, and as he glances back to his fencing, to his driveway ... the front door opens.

Blake steps back in shock upon recognising himself, his past self, leave the house, pulling something heavy with him. Bewildered at what he's witnessing, he watches as he sees his slightly younger self, going by the dark brown hair, drag a suitcase out awkwardly like it weighs a ton. He watches himself take a breath, which radiates visibly from his mouth with the cold temperature. He pauses at the door, glancing back inside, then grabs at the handle of the suitcase again, continuing to drag it down the driveway. As Blake watches, the scenario presented before him starts to fade, and all around is replaced by a house interior; a living room, where a single lamp in one corner is the only light.

"Maybe we should go back a short while earlier." A deep, rumbling voice then says, and Blake looks around but appears to be alone.

"Who... who said that?" He urges nervously.

Origin

"You hold secrets, long buried. It is time that you faced them." The voice continues.

Another voice joins the other, and Blake looks to the open door leading into a hallway, recognising his own.

"Honey?"

Blake walks out to the hallway and witnesses himself hang a jacket on a hook. He then steps aside as his younger self ventures past him into the living room, and watches himself as he looks around, spotting a mug of coffee on a table beside the sofa. Approaching, the other him picks it up, frowning confusion.

On returning to the hallway, Blake watches himself climb the staircase until he stops at seeing Eleanor standing at the top. Emotions threaten to overwhelm Blake as he looks at her, his wife, her mousy brown hair, natural beauty, wearing a dressing gown … he can hardly believe his eyes.

"Darren. Where have you been?" She asks accusingly, her expression stern.

The other-him stares at her as he answers, "Oh, you know how it is hun, long day on the job. A few of the guys wanted to go for some beers."

He goes to ascend and brush past her until he hears a melody play. Eleanor then holds up a cell phone as they stand together at the top of the stairs.

"Think you better answer that, sweetie." She says.

Blake suddenly goes cold. *This is that night,* he thinks, *the last time I ever saw Eleanor.*

The other him then takes out another phone from inside his jacket and looks at the screen.

Eleanor waves her cell at him.

Craig Micklewright

"Think I wouldn't find out? Why you got two phones you son-of-a-bitch?!"

"Now relax, it's not what it looks like."

Eleanor ends the call.

"You know, I was tempted to ring earlier, but I needed to see the look on your face!" - Eleanor then storms away onto the upstairs hallway, and the other him rushes after her.

"Eleanor packed her bag that night. What happened after that, Blake?" the deep voice then interrupts.

Blake starts to slowly ascend the staircase, his head racing. He's unable to think clearly.

"She… she left me."

"Oh, she did, did she? Is that what you told everyone? That your wife walked out of your life?"

"Yes! 'Cause that's what happened!" Blake snaps, steadying himself on the handrail a few steps up.

After a moment, Eleanor's voice is heard, "You disgust me, Darren. You're an embarrassment of a husband. I'm going to my mothers. We'll talk about this when I've calmed down."

Eleanor re-appears at the top of the stairs having changed into jeans and a sweater, and has a large, packed suitcase with her. Blake looks up to her as his other-self joins her where the staircase turns a corner, and sees that he's crying and sniffing up a running nose as he reaches a hand out.

Origin

Blake puts a hand to his temple, a pain suddenly surfacing as behind, the cloaked demon stands in the hallway, "Why are you showing me this?!??" Blake exclaims, tears developing.

The demon lingers in the hallway, "Because you must face your past ... your true past."

Blake sees himself and Eleanor struggle on the staircase. She slaps his face, which stuns the other him and briefly they just stand looking at one another. Eleanor then goes to descend the steps just as he retaliates, shoving her from behind to cause her to lose her footing. Suddenly she falls down the stairs, crying out as Blake staggers out of the way, and watches her tumble then land awkwardly at the bottom - motionless. He backs off to the living room, seeing himself hurry down the stairs and stop where Eleanor now lies. The other-him crouches down and applies a hand to her neck. Then with distress, he falls back against the bottom step, clearly horrified - a reaction mirrored by Blake as he collides with the hallway wall.

"No... it's a lie... you're trying to fool me." He remarks.

The demon looks over to him, "If only that were the truth, Blake. No. What you did that night, formed much of the person you are today... who you have become. You buried your grief and your guilt behind a lie. A lie you told to the rest of the world... for long enough, that you eventually believed it yourself."

"No!!" Blake cries, falling to his knees, and begins to crawl towards Eleanor as the other-him staggers away, panic stricken ... yet before Blake can touch Eleanor's hand, it's

Craig Micklewright

like everything switches to fast forward, and he sits up to witness a speeded-up scene.

His other-self empties the suitcase, discarding her packed clothing, before placing her body within, tucking her in tight then closing and zipping up the case until it bulges. He then hurries out of the house, returning seconds later to lift and drag the suitcase through the front door and down the driveway to his awaiting Sedan.

Blake lingers in the doorway of his house, watching powerlessly at the revelation of his actions, as he places the suitcase, places Eleanor in the trunk then slams it shut.

"God, please no… it can't be." He whimpers, tears streaming until the area around him transforms into dense woodland and he watches his car arrive at a clearing, as he gets out, retrieves the suitcase and goes about digging a grave.

Blake turns away, unable to watch any longer.

"Seen enough?" The demon asks.

Supporting himself against a tree, Blake tries to regain his composure, whilst delving one hand into his over coat. The demon approaches from behind.

"You are a coward, Blake, an impotent excuse of a human. Weak to your own inadequacies. Your own worst enemy. You can't hope to stop this, what has been foretold, for centuries… you are just one person, and a severely damaged one at that."

He reaches Blake, and a snort of his bovine features causes hot breath to hit the back of Blake's neck.

"Except your defeat. You cannot hope to stop me."

Origin

Blake sighs, eyes initially closed tight until he opens them, "Thankfully, it's not about you, ya fuckin' egomaniac!"

Suddenly he unsheathes the jewel-encrusted dagger, turns, and thrusts it deep into the demon's chest. Convulsing, the demon falls down as Blake lunges at him, driving the blade deeper.

"Tell me where she is you piece of shit! Tell me!!"

The hood on the demon falls back to reveal its horns and full goat-like features, yellow eyes glowing. It fights for breath.

"Eleanor has passed over, she... she cannot be reached."

"I know that now asshole. I'm talking about Lisa. Lisa Watts! You have her, you've had her all this time, haven't you? Tell me where! Tell me!"

The demon begins to chuckle, "Think saving that whore's soul can bring you... redemption?" It laughs some more, "You are beyond saving, and so is she."

"We'll see about that!" Blake retorts, twisting the blade until the demon stops breathing, eyes wide and still, and their glow slowly fades. Gradually, Blake gets back up, looking around then notices he's now in a long stone corridor, walls towering endlessly above.

With the dagger held limp in one hand, demon blood dripping from it, he starts to walk forward, hoping and praying that he finds her... finds Lisa, and somehow free her from whatever torment that bastard's subjected her to.

Craig Micklewright

8

Harry stands in the emergency department of a local hospital, talking to a black Police officer.

"You should have brought this to us sooner, Harry. There'll probably be an inquest now." The officer says.

"If you guys had your finger on the pulse these days, you'd have already been aware a devil worshiping cult was operating in this city." Harry retorts defensively.

"Regardless, I guess you're due a thank you. Juanita Equarez and the big guy... Django..."

"Drago."

"... have been on and off our radar but we were unaware of just what they were involved in. Even so, a young man died tonight, so this'll go to trial regardless."

Harry thinks better than to mention Blake. As far as this town is concerned, he's been dead for years, and now he's someone else entirely.

263

Origin

"At least." Harry adds, then a doctor emerges from one of the cubical curtains.

They both look over as Harry chooses to approach.

"Lieutenant Benning." The doctor says in recognition.

"Retired these days Doc. Even if old habits die hard." Harry responds.

"Sorry, Harry... er, your girl, she's asking for someone called 'Blake'."

Harry pulls the doctor aside, away from the officer, "Er, that'll be a friend of ours. He's... not here right now. So, how she doing?"

"After a few transfusions she's going to pull through I'd say, but it was touch and go for a moment."

Harry watches the officer talking on a radio obliviously. He looks back to the doctor.

"May I see her?"

"Sure. She's still quite weak mind, so I'd not stay long if I were you. She's gonna need rest."

Eventually, Harry enters the cubical to see Gemma sitting propped up on a bed, hooked up to an I.V. She's white as a sheet and has been changed into a hospital gown.

"Hey kid, how you feeling?"

Gemma sighs, looking to Harry briefly before looking away.

Harry comes to the bedside, looking down at her, "Yeah I know. I'm really sorry about your brother."

"Forget about it." She says quietly.

264

Craig Micklewright

Harry sits on the edge of the bed and looks at her sternly, "Blake... he's er..." - Gemma looks at him again as he recognises concern in her hazel eyes.

"He's missing." He continues, "He er, vanished as we were all getting out of that place. I think you'd passed out by then."

"What do you mean he… vanished?"

Harry looks down at himself, trying not to think the worst, "I… I don't know. One second he was there and then…"

"He wasn't?"

He looks at the young girl again, appreciating that in the whole mess of things, at least she had survived. He reaches forward to touch her hand.

"But I'm going to find him, Gemma. If it's the last thing I do."

Gemma turns her hand in his and returns a tight squeeze.

"You better had." She replies adamantly.

*

Blood drips from Blake's hand. It was as if he'd been walking for hours, even though the concept of time felt different in such a place. Stopping in his tracks, he winces in pain as his hand pulses for the first time since the dagger drew his blood at Lisa's grave. Looking to his bandaged left hand, blood soaks through the fabric covering his palm. He conceals the dagger back inside his coat and unravels the bandage slowly, revealing a grisly open wound. It appears far worse than it had been up until now, as blood drips from it

Origin

copiously. Blake glances to the ground and notices a small pool having formed. *What the hell?* He thinks.

As he stares at the pool, the blood starts to congeal and separate before his eyes, gradually forming a word: 'Darren'. Blake steps away in disbelief, then as he continues to observe the blood, the letters transform again, forming the word: 'Save' and finally the word: 'Me'.

Suddenly, the blood comes together, then shoots off down the long, stone corridor. Blake doesn't think, he just hurries after it, picking up pace until he's sprinting.

Blake skids around the corner at the end of the corridor, then freezes as he sees what appears to be a cell door with iron bars in a small window. Pausing to look, he then jolts as a figure comes to it, hands gripped to the bars - its Eleanor.

"Blake, how could you? I died with nobody ever knowing. You stole their grief. Leaving everyone to just wonder about me, forever."

Blake approaches the door, reaching to the bars and touches Eleanor's fingers.

"El… I am so sorry, please, find a way to forgive me."

Eleanor's mouth then forms a wicked grin as her mousy brown hair transforms into striking white. Suddenly Blake is presented with the face of Sarah, his fiancé, complete with that fixed, jagged-toothed grin. Her eyes glow a bright yellow.

"You're not Eleanor!" Blake retorts, backing off, "You're not Sarah neither. You're just trying to fuck with me!"

Blake then hears a voice, distant, female, "Darren?" it calls.

Craig Micklewright

He looks down the corridor, leaving Sarah to quietly chuckle, and notices the blood has created a red, glistening line along the stone wall opposite, leading onwards. Blake follows, hurrying forward until he reaches the end to discover corridors heading in three more directions; left, right and straight ahead. Looking to the wall, the blood drips onto the floor, then begins to draw another line that forms into an arrow, pointing in the direction of the facing corridor. With a build up of nerves, Blake walks forward, scared but also hopeful of where the corridor might lead as he contemplates who or what has been guiding him.

Outside the hospital, Harry walks up to Widow as she stands leaning against a railing, finishing a cigarette.

"You're still here?" He asks her.

Briefly he looks to the sky, noticing how the full moon has a slight shadow on it, the eclipse having passed. Despite his growing concerns over Blake, in all other aspects it was like the whole world had just dodged a bullet – without even knowing it.

"Is she going to be alright?" Widow asks, dropping and treading out her cigarette under a Doc Martin boot.

"You did well, stopping the bleeding." Harry answers, "She may not realise it, but you probably saved her life. She's gonna be fine. I just spoke to her. That kid has some grieving ahead of her but, she's strong."

Widow sighs then pushes herself away from the railing.

"Where you off? Do you want me to drop you somewhere?" Harry asks as he watches her walk away.

267

Origin

Widow glances back, "Nah, thanks. Er, I guess I've got a lot of thinking to do. I appreciate you not saying anything to the cops."

Harry smiles back, watching her leave, before slowly heading for the hospital car park to where his trusty old Volvo awaits him.

Blake enters a vast room, which resembles a cathedral. Tall, stained-glass windows either side beam in a misty multi-coloured light. In the centre of the room stands a large cage, and this is where the blood has been leading him. Hurrying over, Blake takes the dagger from his coat and starts to hack at a flesh-like substance covering the lock. Cutting it away as more blood splashes against him, eventually the flesh falls away and he grips a handle, pulling a rusted iron door open. Inside, presented on a stone slab, lies the naked body of a woman, jet-black hair hanging down either side. Reaching the slab as he discards the dagger, Blake casts his eyes on the face of Lisa Watts. Bringing his hand to her cheek, he cradles her face to his palm as emotions build inside him.

"Lisa. I'm here, baby. It's… It's Darren." – *damn, she hasn't aged a day*, he observes.

Slowly, Lisa starts to stir, at first her lips quiver and her eyes move beneath their lids. Blake moves his hand to stroke her hair, watching with bated breath. Her eyes then spring open, and she looks to him as she opens her mouth.

"Darren?" She says weakly and as she sits up, he embraces her just as she wraps an arm around his shoulder, hearing him weep.

268

Suddenly a voice booms through the room, "Really think it would be that easy?"

Blake lifts his head, before moving away from Lisa and looks outside of the cage to see a shuffling, severely weakened Nefalym approach.

"You…" Blake remarks with hatred, and just as he goes to retrieve the dagger from the floor, Lisa grabs his arm.

Blake looks to her as she climbs off the slab, long black hair flowing longer than he remembered, down her back to the cheeks of her ass. She walks in front of him, newly empowered.

"No, Darren. He's mine." She says then walks out from the cage holding one arm out, the fingers of her hand splayed open.

Nefalym looks at her then starts to shake and convulse. He staggers on his hoofed feet, but Lisa has him in some sort of ethereal grip,

"This can not be!" He groans.

Lisa stares to him sternly, "You made me what I am. Now suffer the consequences!" She says back, forcing his body into a violent seizure.

Behind, Blake follows Lisa out to watch. Then as he sees the goat-like demon jolting and shaking, all of a sudden… Nefalym explodes.

As if drained of her power, Lisa drops to her knees as body parts, guts and flesh rain down. Blake comes to her aid, enveloping her in his arms as she turns to him, and he holds her head to his chest.

"It's ok, it's ok. I've got you." He says, holding her tight.

Origin

After a moment, she raises her head and Blake meets it with a kiss to her lips, a kiss that progresses as they lie down together and he caresses her, trailing kisses down her neck as he runs a hand along her body. Lisa groans as he kisses and mouths her breast, and she hooks one leg around him, grasping the back of his head; becoming lovers once again.

"Thank you, Darren." She breathes, and Blake pauses to look at her, just as she slowly fades into a mist beneath him and disappears.

Blake exhales and lowers his head to meet the floor, tears flowing. The pain in his heart at finding her only to lose her all over again, is only eased with the realisation that she's no longer that creature's slave. Lisa can finally rest.

Craig Micklewright

Epilogue

The following morning, Harry's Volvo arrives in the grounds of Townsend Shipping & Storage. The charcoaled shell of the warehouse building stands surrounded by several police squad cars and a forensics van, while particles of ash still linger in the air - a grim reminder of the previous night's blaze.

Exiting his vehicle, Harry surveys the building before heading toward a group of chatting police officers.

"Harry? What are you doing here?" asks one, biting into a donut.

"He was here last night. He's the reason we have that Equarez woman and her goon in custody." another officer chimes in, holding a plastic cup of coffee.

Approaching them, Harry gestures toward the building, "Morning, fellas. So, did you find anything else in this carcass?"

Origin

The officer with the coffee shakes his head, "Nah man, other than that shirtless dude from last night - 'fraid he's been cooked better than my Momma's Sunday roast. He'll have to be officially identified."

Harry sighs, conflicted by the news. *If Blake wasn't there, then where the hell is he?*

"Well, I presume that guy's sister will be able to do that, once she's recovered." He adds.

"Is it true what they're saying, sir?" the donut-eating officer asks, catching Harry's attention, "That it was some kind of satanic ritual?"

Harry lowers his head, "I wouldn't like to comment… guess that's for those two whack jobs to fill you boys in on."

He then turns away, walking toward the entrance of the warehouse. The since melted shutters offer a view into a vast interior. His gaze falls upon where the altar had been, now cordoned off with police tape. With another sigh, he turns away and heads back to his Volvo.

Sitting in silence, he ponders recent events. *Damn it, Blake… what happened?*

Retrieving his cell phone from his jacket, he scrolls through a list of contacts before stopping at the one he's looking for: Patricia. Hesitating for numerous reasons, he finally brings up her profile and presses the call icon.

*

Blake opens his eyes as he feels heat burning down on him, accompanied by a gentle breeze. Raising his head he finds himself on a building site. Standing up, feeling a little

Craig Micklewright

unsteady, he makes his way out from the framework of a partially erected building. Proceeding towards the street, he passes workmen using machinery, building walls and chatting obliviously amongst themselves.

As traffic whizzes by, he notices how warm it is and that the city looks vibrant and alive, especially jarring for Springdale. There's something strangely unfamiliar about the place.

Blake crosses the road and heads onto another street, walking along a row of shops. A bus passes, an advert for the movie 'Avengers: Infinity War' displayed on its side. Feeling increasingly bewildered and disoriented he proceeds by a convenience store, catching the eye of a girl inside standing behind the counter, looking at him with curiosity until a customer approaches.

Gemma, her hair in a ponytail, wearing a uniform, serves a middle-aged woman, helping to pack the groceries as she glances again to the window. For a moment she feels a familiarity to the guy who was just outside, but whoever it was, has now gone.

"Will that be everything?" She asks as she returns her attention to the customer.

Blake reaches the street corner and hails a cab, waving his left hand out until a yellow taxi pulls up before him. For a moment he looks at his hand and notices the cut has disappeared. Not pondering the discovery any longer, he climbs in the back to see a Mexican-looking man at the wheel.

"Where to, señor?"

Origin

"Greenwich, please."

The driver adjusts the gears and treads down on the gas, as Blake relaxes back. Lisa is still very much at the forefront of his thoughts. He can still feel the warmth of her skin, can still taste the moisture of her lips. Such a loss will clearly stay with him just like it did the last time, even if now it was all wrapped in a blanket of bittersweet closure.

Shortly afterwards the cab arrives outside a brownstone apartment building in Greenwich Village. Climbing out and paying the driver, Blake looks up to the building as the cab leaves. He then spots Harry's Volvo parked out front. It's a reassuring sight until he notices that it's on bricks and has no wheels, closer inspection revealing a degree of rust.

Eventually he exits an elevator and heads along the corridor before reaching a door. He raises a hand to knock until he remembers he has a key. Reaching into his over coat, he retrieves his key and pushes it into the lock, turning it to gain entry. Almost as soon as he enters, a little girl comes running towards him wearing a pink onesie that makes her look like a rabbit. At first thinking he's entered the wrong apartment, Blake pins his back to the door as the little girl reaches him, looking up with large brown eyes that match curly brown hair.

"Er… hi." He remarks uncomfortably, then looks past her to see Harry exit the living area. On seeing Blake, Harry almost cries out in shock.

"Oh, hi Harry, so… you gonna introduce us?" Blake asks referring to the girl who lingers by Blake's legs.

Craig Micklewright

"Blake!?!" Harry exclaims in astonishment.

Blake returns a confused look, "Yeah, you ok Harry?"

Harry looks different, like he's lost weight and just stands there, flabbergasted as just then, Patricia exits the living area in mid-speech.

"Harry, did you see Jess' come out here…"

She turns and sees Blake, her mouth falling open. Suddenly she rushes to him. The little girl scurries over to Harry as Patricia embraces an increasingly confused Blake.

"Blake! Oh my God! Is it really you?"

Blake returns her embrace, holding her tightly around the waist as she squeezes him with affection. Her reaction to seeing him almost brings a tear to his eye, considering what she said to him in that *place*.

"Patricia… what are you doing here, and who's this?" He asks.

Patricia let's go of him; her face flushed. She's so happy to see him, and notices how he's looking to the little girl.

"I've just been visiting for a few days." She answers, "This is Jessica, remember?"

"I don't get it, she was just… a baby."

Patricia's brow wrinkles at his response, and she looks back to Harry.

"You've been gone for over three years, Blake." Harry then announces, walking slowly forward, looking like he's seen a ghost.

Blake can't comprehend what he's hearing, even though the evidence is presented before him. Patricia appears fresh-faced, her hair once again long and she looks content and happy.

Origin

"I… I think I need a drink."

Patricia looks at him some more as if to make sure he's real, then Jessica comes to her side; so little she barely reaches Patricia's waist. Dropping her hand to take Jessica's, Patricia smiles at her before refocusing on Blake.

"Jess, honey. This is your Uncle Blake." She says, and the little girl looks up at him before hiding behind her mother's leg.

"Oh don't mind her, she can be a tad shy."

Blake just returns a nervous smile.

On entering his room minutes later, he see's the sofa bed folded up, and there's a number of boxes and piles of magazines littering the floor and on a chest of drawers. Perusing one of the magazine covers, he realises they're all about the paranormal. Clearly Harry was doing some research, and going by the amount of stuff that is piled in the room, it was bordering on an obsession. Blake looks away and opens a wardrobe, seeing some clothing still hanging there. Reaching inside his coat, he takes out the dagger - still stained in blood, now dry and crusty on the blade. He proceeds to hide the dagger on a top shelf amongst some towels, before closing the door. Again, he looks at his hand, running his fingers over the area where the cut had been - there's not even a scar remaining. Having seen and done enough to stop him questioning strange occurrences, he looks back to the open bedroom door. *Oh well, back to the twilight zone*, he thinks to himself and returns to the hallway.

Craig Micklewright

On entering the living area, Patricia is kneeling on the floor, playing with Jessica where a collection of toys are spread. With an intake of breath, he walks over to the sofa and slumps down opposite Harry who is in his armchair. So begins Blake's task of trying to explain where he has been for the last three years. Sitting there, looking to the two closest people in his life, he realises he couldn't be in better company. The question of whether he's actually deserving of their friendship however, remains something he may never want answering.

Many thanks for reading 'Origin'

This novel I consider my most ambitious writing project to date. Built on the foundation that was my previous novel, *Forever Midnight*, I'd say this is a more complex, multi-layered story, with a number of challenging sequences that I feel develop me as a writer. I'm immensely proud of how it has turned out and hope that you got as much out of reading it as I did writing it.

The ideas behind Origin have been in my head for a number of years, and I wanted to further explore Blake / Darren, originally introduced in *The Dying Game*, who is a complex and flawed person for whom this story gradually reveals all his personal demons and psychological intricacies. At the same time, with the character, Lisa Watts only occasionally featured in Forever Midnight, for a long time I'd been wanting to fully reveal what happened to her as well. Put these two together and you have *Origin*.

Please seek out my other novels and if so obliged, leave me a review over on **Amazon**.

Craig.

ii

Printed in Dunstable, United Kingdom